Shadow of the Lost

SHADOW OF THE LOST

A Guardians Adventure

Book 1

BENJAMIN HINES

Publishing the Voice of Southern Appalachia

ISBN 9798341222557

First Edition

For My Son

Your courage is in the choice you make to do the thing that is right, even though it scares you.

I see your courage.

You make me proud.

Prologue
The Chase

The roar of the ATV engine echoed through the dense forest, leaves and branches whipping past as Deacon gripped the handlebars tighter, his knuckles white. His best friend, Sean, clung to the back of the vehicle, his eyes wide as they bounced over rocks and roots. Behind them, the snarling sound of dirt bikes grew louder. They were getting closer.

"Faster, Deacon!" Sean shouted, his voice nearly drowned out by the wind and the engine's growl.

"I'm trying!" Deacon yelled back, swerving hard to avoid a fallen tree. The ATV skidded, tires kicking up dirt and pine needles as they rounded a sharp bend in the trail. Deacon's heart pounded in rhythm with the machine beneath him, but it wasn't just adrenaline. It was the small, wooden box stuffed in his backpack—the box that had somehow turned their lives upside down.

"Why do they want this thing so badly?" Sean asked, his voice tinged with panic.

Deacon didn't have an answer. All he knew was that the moment he had grabbed the box from that underground vault, the chase had started. And the guys after them? They weren't the friendly type.

The dirt bikes revved louder, closer. Too close. Deacon glanced over his shoulder just in time to see one of the riders—masked, all in black—reach for something. A flash of metal. A gun?

"Hold on!" Deacon veered off the trail, plunging the ATV down a steep embankment. Sean let out a terrified yelp as they shot through the underbrush, the trees a blur of green and brown. The ATV bucked and lurched beneath them, threatening to throw them off at any second, but Deacon managed to keep them upright.

Behind them, the dirt bikes struggled to follow, but one of the riders was more determined than the others. He barreled down after them, gaining ground.

Deacon's heart sank as the trees ahead thinned, revealing a sheer drop—a cliff, looming like the end of the world.

"Uh, Deacon," Sean said, his voice shaky, "that's a cliff!"

"I see it!" Deacon shouted back, skidding to a halt just feet from the edge. He killed the engine, the ATV sputtering out, leaving only the distant rumble of the dirt bikes and the churning rapids below.

"No, no, no... this can't be it," Sean muttered, pacing in frantic circles. "We're stuck!"

Deacon whipped around. The masked rider was already closing in, his bike roaring through the trees. They had seconds—maybe less.

Deacon's mind raced. They couldn't outrun him, not with the cliff behind them. His eyes darted over the cliff's edge. There—a narrow ledge, just visible, maybe a few feet down.

"Sean, grab the ATV! Help me push!"

"What? Are you crazy?"

"Trust me!"

Sean hesitated, then nodded, throwing his weight into the ATV. Together, they pushed it toward the cliff's edge. The dirt bike's engine screamed louder. The rider was almost on top of them.

"Now!" Deacon shouted. They heaved the ATV over the edge, watching it tumble and crash onto the ledge below. Without another word, they scrambled down after it, their fingers clawing at the rock.

They crouched in silence, hearts pounding, hidden just below the cliff's lip as the masked rider skidded to a stop at the top. Deacon held his breath, every muscle tense, praying the rider wouldn't spot them.

The masked man cursed under his breath, scanning the horizon, unaware that the boys were just feet below him. "The Order is not going to like this."

Then, after a long, agonizing moment, he revved the engine and sped off into the trees.

Deacon exhaled, his body sagging with relief. But as he glanced at Sean, who was equally breathless and wide-eyed, one thought gnawed at him: Who were these guys? And what was in the box?

One thing was clear—they were in way over their heads.

And the worst part?

This was only the beginning.

Chapter 1
The Inheritance

10 Days Earlier - California

The sun hung low in the California sky, casting a warm, golden hue over the quiet suburban street as Deacon Koster pedaled his bike up the driveway of his foster home. He always felt a small sense of relief at this moment every day—the routine, the stability. It wasn't always like this, bouncing from one foster home to another after his parents' accident.

He paused for a moment, letting the familiar scene wash over him—Bob's well-maintained lawn, the American flag flapping gently in the breeze, the smell of Judy's cooking drifting through the open kitchen window. This was home. And it wasn't just because he lived here. Bob and Judy made sure he felt like this was home. He wasn't just another kid passing through; they treated him like family.

Bob, a retired Navy SEAL, had spent countless weekends teaching Deacon everything he knew about the water—how to scuba dive, how to pilot a boat, and all about marine life. Sometimes it felt like Bob was grooming him to be an oceanographer, or maybe just making sure he'd never be afraid of the deep. Deacon had grown to love those weekends on the water, the cool ocean spray on his face, and the sound of the waves slapping against the hull of Bob's small boat.

Judy, a former ER nurse, had her own ideas about what every kid should know—basic first aid. Whenever Deacon scraped himself playing basketball or wiped out on his skateboard, Judy didn't just patch him up; she made him learn how to do it himself. She'd talk him through how to treat a sprain or set a broken bone. "It's not just about knowing it," she'd say, "it's about being calm when you have to use it."

Deacon smiled at the thought as he leaned his bike against the garage, pausing for a moment to breathe in the scent of freshly cut grass and Judy's lasagna wafting through the open kitchen window. It had been a long day at school—quizzes, a chemistry lab that went sideways, and Sean's endless chatter about the latest conspiracy theory video he found on YouTube. But now, he could unwind.

He swung open the front door, calling out, "I'm home!" But instead of the familiar sound of Judy humming in the kitchen or Bob watching the news, he heard low voices coming from the living room.

That was odd.

Dropping his backpack near the door, Deacon cautiously made his way down the hall. When he stepped into the living room, he froze. A man he didn't recognize was sitting in one of the armchairs—a man who looked like he'd stepped out of a high-end magazine ad. He was in his late thirties, with blonde hair neatly combed back and a tailored suit that fit him like a glove. Despite his polished appearance, there was a hint of discomfort in his posture, as if he didn't enjoy being the bearer of bad news. His slate grey eyes, although almost colorless, held a certain warmth that softened the intensity of his presence.

Sean was perched on the arm of the couch, wide-eyed as

ever, and Bob and Judy sat across from the stranger, their faces unusually serious.

The man stood up as Deacon entered. "You must be Deacon Koster," he said, extending his hand. His voice was smooth, professional, but not cold.

"Yeah," Deacon said slowly, taking the man's hand. "That's me."

"I'm Mr. Oliver," the man continued, his grip firm but brief. "I'm an attorney. I've come on behalf of your uncle, Tecumseh Koster. I believe you knew him as 'Cump.'"

Deacon blinked, the words not quite landing. My uncle? He didn't have an uncle. Or at least, not one he knew about.

Mr. Oliver must have seen the confusion on Deacon's face because he paused, looking from Deacon to Bob and Judy, clearly sensing something was off. "I'm sure this must be a shock to you but…"

"No," Deacon interrupted, shaking his head. "My... uncle?" Deacon's stomach dropped. "I don't—" He paused, glancing at Bob and Judy, hoping they'd jump in with some kind of explanation, but their faces remained carefully neutral. "I didn't even know I had an uncle."

Mr. Oliver exhaled softly, as if the weight of the conversation had just doubled. "I see. Well, I'm afraid I have some unexpected news for you. Your uncle passed away recently and left you an inheritance."

Sean let out a low whistle from the couch. "Whoa, man. That's wild."

Deacon shot him a look, still trying to process what was happening. "Wait... what kind of inheritance? Why me?"

Mr. Oliver reached into his briefcase and pulled out a thick, neatly folded envelope, placing it on the coffee table between them. "Your uncle left very specific instructions. You are to inherit his estate—a large property in a small town called Ashebridge, North Carolina."

"Ashebridge?" Deacon echoed, his mind racing. He didn't know anything about this place, or this uncle.

"There is, however, a condition," Mr. Oliver said carefully, his slate-grey eyes locking onto Deacon's. "The only way you can claim the inheritance is if you move there. Permanently."

Deacon's heart pounded in his chest. Move? Leave Bob and Judy? Leave California? Leave everything?

"What? Like, move there now?" he asked, his voice a mix of disbelief and frustration.

Mr. Oliver nodded. "Yes. In order to inherit the property, you have to reside on it. The estate cannot be sold, transferred, or rented. It's yours only if you live there."

Deacon sank into the nearest chair, running a hand through his hair. This was unreal. Just a few minutes ago, he was thinking about dinner and basketball. Now he was being told to leave everything behind, to move across the country to claim some inheritance from an uncle he never even knew existed.

Sean, who had been unusually quiet for a while, suddenly straightened up, a look of realization crossing his face. "Hey, uh, you know, I saw this video once about… what's it called? Like, when you're, uh, legally an adult before you're 18. You can, like, live on your own and stuff."

Mr. Oliver, helpfully supplied, "Yes, legal emancipation. That's the term."

"Yeah! That's it," Sean nodded, snapping his fingers. "Emancipation. I bet I could apply for it. I'm almost 17, right? And my foster family's pretty chill, they'd probably be cool with it. Then… I could come with you. You wouldn't have to do this alone."

Deacon stared at his best friend, part of him wanting to

laugh at the absurdity of the idea, but the other part—well, the other part felt a little relieved. Of course Sean had been watching some weird video about legal loopholes. But the fact that he was already thinking of a way to come with him made Deacon's chest tighten. Sean was always there. Always.

Mr. Oliver cleared his throat again, clearly trying to stay professional but uncomfortable with the weight of the conversation. "You don't need to decide immediately. You have a few weeks to make your decision. But after three weeks, the estate will go to another beneficiary if you choose not to claim it."

Deacon stared at the envelope on the table, his mind a whirl of emotions. Part of him wanted to tear it open, to figure out why this mysterious uncle had left him everything. But another part of him—probably the bigger part—wanted to pretend this conversation never happened.

Bob's voice cut through the silence. "Listen, Deacon," he said, leaning forward. His voice was calm, steady, like it always was. "No matter what you decide, we're proud of you. This is your decision to make, and we'll support you either way."

Judy nodded, her eyes full of quiet understanding. "You've got a good head on your shoulders, sweetheart. Whatever you choose, you'll make the right call."

Deacon appreciated their words, but the weight of the decision still pressed down on him. He had always thought his life would take a certain path—finish high school, maybe go to college, figure out who he really was. But now? Everything had changed in a single afternoon.

Sean nudged him with his elbow. "Come on, man. Think of it as an adventure."

Deacon sighed, his gaze drifting to the envelope on the table. Adventure wasn't exactly the word he would use. But deep down, something tugged at him—a curiosity, a spark. Who was this uncle? Why did he leave all of this to him? And why did it feel like this decision was bigger than just an estate? It felt bigger than that—like there was something he didn't quite understand yet, but he'd have to figure it out soon.

Chapter 2
The Decision

The rhythmic thud of the basketball echoed in the still afternoon air as Deacon dribbled slowly, each bounce a steady beat against the concrete. He stood alone on the cracked asphalt court in the backyard, eyes scanning the worn hoop above him. The rim wobbled slightly from years of use, but it was still good enough to shoot on. His mind was racing, though, not just about the next shot.

A few days had passed since Mr. Oliver's visit, but the decision that lay in front of him felt no clearer. Moving to North Carolina. Leaving behind everything—his school, his friends, the basketball team he'd spent years building chemistry with. His first taste of stability in years, thanks to Bob and Judy, now felt like it was being ripped away by someone he hadn't even known existed.

He dribbled the ball absentmindedly, his thoughts tugging at him in a hundred different directions. It wasn't like he had a bad life here. He liked his school, his teammates. He wasn't the star player, but he was good enough to contribute, good enough to feel like he was part of something. The idea of leaving all that behind twisted in his chest.

But there was something else, too. A part of him had always felt like there was something more waiting for him out there. Something bigger than California, bigger than the life he'd known. He couldn't explain it, but the pull was there. This strange inheritance, this mysterious uncle—it was like a puzzle, a challenge calling to him from the unknown.

He stopped dribbling, gripping the ball tightly as he stared up at the hoop. What if this was his shot? A once-in-a-lifetime chance to uncover something about his family, about himself?

Still, how would he even make it work? He was only sixteen. And Bob and Judy—how could he leave them behind after everything they'd done for him? They weren't just foster parents. They were his real family, in every way that mattered. He didn't want them to think he didn't appreciate everything they'd done.

Sighing, Deacon tossed the ball toward the hoop, watching as it bounced off the rim and rolled away. He wiped a hand across his face. He needed answers.

Pulling his phone from his pocket, Deacon scrolled through his contacts until he found Mr. Oliver's number. His thumb hovered over the call button for a moment before he pressed it, bringing the phone to his ear. It rang twice before a familiar smooth voice answered.

"Deacon," Mr. Oliver said. "I wasn't expecting to hear from you so soon."

Deacon paused, unsure where to start. "I've been thinking about what you said. About moving to North Carolina. I don't even know how it would work. I'm still a minor."

There was a brief silence before Mr. Oliver replied, his tone softer than it had been the first time they met. "I understand this is a big decision, Deacon. I'm here to help you through it. Your uncle appointed me as the trustee of his estate, which means

I'll be here to assist you with anything you need—finances, legal matters, you name it."

Deacon hesitated. "And what about… getting there? I can't just pack up and leave."

Mr. Oliver's voice carried a touch of warmth. "We can expedite the process for your emancipation. It's not as complicated as it sounds, and I'll be here to handle the paperwork and make sure everything goes smoothly. Your uncle made provisions for everything."

Deacon bit his lip. "Emancipation… you mean I'd be legally on my own?"

"In a way, yes," Mr. Oliver replied. "But you wouldn't be alone. I'd still be here to manage the estate and help you make decisions, especially while you're getting settled. And, if it helps, I've already spoken to Sean's foster family. They and his social worker are supportive of him seeking emancipation as well. I'd be happy to assist with his paperwork if he's planning to go with you."

Deacon's stomach twisted. Sean. Of course, Sean would want to come with him. He was loyal to a fault, never letting Deacon face anything on his own.

"Thanks, Mr. Oliver," Deacon said finally. "I need to think about it."

"Of course. Take your time. But remember, you have two more weeks before we'll need your decision."

Deacon hung up and stared at his phone, his thoughts churning. Was it even right for him to leave? Bob and Judy had invested so much love into him. And his basketball team—they were counting on him this season. Would they think he was abandoning them?

He grabbed the basketball again, feeling the familiar weight in his hands. Maybe he couldn't make the decision himself.

Maybe he'd let fate decide.

Taking a deep breath, Deacon walked to the three-point line and set his feet. "Okay," he muttered to himself, "if I make three three-pointers in a row, I'll go. If not, I stay."

He dribbled the ball, feeling the smooth texture under his fingers before he squared up and released. The ball arced perfectly, swishing through the net.

"One," Deacon whispered, jogging to retrieve the ball.

He returned to the line, taking his time with the second shot. Another swish.

His heart raced as he lined up for the third. His hands were steady, his mind focused. He released. The ball sailed cleanly through the net again.

"Three." Deacon's breath caught in his throat. That had to be a fluke, he thought. He'd never shot that well before, not three in a row. He wasn't ready to decide yet.

"Okay," he said aloud, pacing the court. "Five shots. From five different spots." He nodded to himself, setting the new terms.

Deacon moved to a different spot on the court and shot again. Another swish. Then again, from the corner. Swish. Two more, from each wing—both swishes. His final shot came from dead center. He squared up, took a deep breath, and let it fly.

The ball sailed in a perfect arc and dropped cleanly through the hoop.

Deacon stood frozen, staring at the hoop in disbelief. He'd never shot like that in his life. It couldn't be random. Could it?

"Well, if that's not a sign, I don't know what is."

Deacon spun around, startled. Sean was leaning against the chain-link fence, arms crossed, grinning like he'd been watching a show.

"You saw all of that?" Deacon asked, his voice cracking

slightly.

"Dude, I saw the last five," Sean said, walking over. "And I gotta say, if that doesn't convince you, nothing will." He gave Deacon a playful shove. "Besides, I'm coming with you, remember? I talked to my foster parents, and they're cool with me getting emancipated. Mr. Oliver's helping with the paperwork and everything."

Deacon blinked at his friend. "You're really serious about this?"

Sean nodded, his expression softening. "You're my family, man. Wherever you go, I'm going, too. Besides, think about it—we could be living in some huge estate in North Carolina. Who knows what kind of adventure we'll get into?"

Deacon chuckled, shaking his head. He didn't know what kind of adventure lay ahead. All he knew was that curiosity was winning the internal battle, slowly pulling him toward something bigger, something unknown.

"Okay," Deacon said finally, his voice barely above a whisper. "Let's do it. Let's go to North Carolina."

But even as the words left his mouth, the question lingered in his mind: Who was this uncle? And why had he left everything to me?

Whatever the answers, Deacon knew one thing for sure—his life would never be the same again.

Chapter 3
Cabin in the Woods

Ashebridge, North Carolina

The cabin was bigger than Sean expected. As they pulled up in the old Jeep Wrangler, the tires crunching over gravel, Sean craned his neck to take in the sprawling property. It was quiet, secluded—like something out of one of those movies where the characters stumble across a hidden treasure, or worse, a ghost.

"Wow," Sean muttered, peering out the window. "This place is legit."

Deacon, sitting behind the wheel, just nodded, his face set in that same serious expression he'd had since they'd left California. Sean could tell he was still processing everything. But, honestly, who could blame him? A secret inheritance, an estate in the middle of nowhere, an uncle no one knew about—it was a lot to handle.

They parked by the cabin, which sat nestled among towering pines. A small lake shimmered in the distance, its surface still and glassy under the late afternoon sun. Several outbuildings dotted the property—old barns, maybe, or storage sheds. The cabin itself was modest, but it looked cozy, with its wooden logs and big windows. There was a porch swing out front on one end of a large porch that partially wrapped around the side of the cabin and wood stacked neatly by the door, as if waiting for someone to come and light a fire.

Sean hopped out of the Jeep, stretching his legs. Apparently, the 4x4 came with the house and Mr. Oliver thought the boys would appreciate the drive in from Charlotte by themselves. So, he arranged to have their new ride waiting for them at the arrivals terminal when they landed at Charlotte Douglas International Airport.

"Man, this place is wild. Like, who knew your uncle was living like some kind of mountain man?"

Deacon shrugged, grabbing his duffel bag from the backseat. "Yeah, I'm still trying to figure that out."

They made their way inside, and Sean immediately noticed how well-kept the place was. It didn't have that abandoned, dusty vibe he half-expected. Instead, the cabin was tidy and furnished with taste. Books lined the walls in nearly every room, from history and physics to ancient mythologies of the world. Some of the shelves were crammed so full that the spines were bending under the weight.

"This dude was definitely a bookworm," Sean said, running his finger along one of the shelves. "Or maybe just obsessed with random stuff."

Deacon gave a faint smile, but Sean could see his friend was preoccupied. This whole place felt mysterious—too mysterious for Deacon's comfort. Deacon picked up a cardboard box labeled "Deacon's Room" and headed towards what he presumed to be his temporary bedroom, with Sean trailing behind him with another box under his arm. The cabin was a blend of cozy living space mixed with what seemed like relics from a lifetime of adventures or eccentricities. Each room they passed hinted at stories untold.

"Woah, what's up with this?" Sean chuckled, stopping abruptly in the hallway to point at a battle axe mounted on the bathroom wall. Its handle was carved with intricate symbols, and the blade gleamed menacingly under the led lights.

Deacon shrugged, his interest piqued despite himself. "Decoration? Or maybe Uncle Cump was into medieval reenactments?"

They continued setting down their belongings in their respective rooms. Sean's room had a desk that overlooked the small lake outside, the serene view clashing with the utilitarian harshness of the steel frame bed beside it. He placed his bag on the bed, opened it, and began to unpack his clothes, setting a few personal items on the desk—a framed photo of him and Deacon, a small, worn-out teddy bear he'd had since he was a kid, and his laptop.

Deacon's room was similar, simple and spartan, with a surprising addition—a pair of night vision goggles lay on the nightstand, looking entirely out of place next to the quaint lamp and the stack of local history books. Deacon picked them up, examining them curiously. They were heavy and professional, not the sort of thing you'd find in a typical household.

"Check this out," Deacon called out, holding them up. Sean peeked his head through the doorway.

"Whoa, was your uncle some kind of secret agent?" Sean joked, but his tone suggested he wasn't entirely kidding.

"With the way things are in this house, I wouldn't be

surprised," Deacon replied, placing the goggles back down with a soft thud.

After setting up their rooms, they ventured into the master bedroom, which held another surprise. The closet was open, revealing a vast array of clothing that ranged from heavy fur-lined coats suitable for Arctic expeditions to lightweight, breathable fabrics perfect for the Sahara. Some clothes looked like they were picked up from local markets in distant countries, vibrant with colors and patterns.

"Looks like Uncle Cump was quite the globetrotter," Deacon murmured, thumbing through the garments. Each piece seemed to carry a scent of the places it had been, a whisper of the life Cump had lived.

The more they explored, the more the cabin felt like a museum of a life well-traveled and enigmatic, filled with artifacts that each held a slice of mystery. It was as if the walls themselves were urging them to dig deeper, to uncover the secrets held within the quiet, wood-lined rooms of the cabin.

The intensity of the cabin was overwhelming. Sean decided to try and lighten the mood. "Hey, you think we're gonna find some kind of treasure map tucked behind these?" He pulled a book from one of the shelves as if to make his point.

But instead of just pulling out a book, the shelf jerked forward slightly. Sean blinked, surprised, as the entire bookcase swung inward with a soft creak.

"Dude, no way…" Sean whispered, stepping back.

Deacon's eyes widened, his earlier seriousness giving way to pure disbelief. "Did you just… open a secret door?"

"I think so?" Sean looked at his hand as if it had done something magical. "I mean, I was joking, but—"

Deacon grabbed his shoulder and pulled him toward the opening. "Come on. Let's see what's inside."

The secret room was small, more like an office than anything else. A single desk sat in the middle, cluttered with papers, notebooks, and what looked like a half-finished cryptogram, the letters and symbols scribbled across the paper in a meticulous but incomplete design. There were maps tacked to the walls, some of them old and yellowed, and others marked with strange annotations in the margins.

Sean's curiosity immediately spiked. "This is like something out of a spy movie," he said, moving toward the desk. "What do you think this cryptogram is?"

Deacon didn't answer, already pulling out his phone and walking back into the main part of the house. "I'm calling Mr. Oliver. Maybe he can tell us something."

While Deacon dialed, Sean flipped through the papers on the desk. His eyes darted over the cryptogram, but the symbols made no sense to him. He reached for a notebook that had been tucked under a pile of documents when something caught his eye—a book wedged between the desk and the wall. It looked like it had been knocked there by accident, just barely out of sight.

Sean knelt down and fished it out. The title read The Culper Spy Ring.

"Hey, check this out," Sean said, holding up the book for Deacon to see. But Deacon was too absorbed in his conversation with Mr. Oliver to pay attention and already walking out of sight.

Sean shrugged and opened the book. The pages were old, slightly yellowed, but what really stood out were the underlined letters scattered throughout the text. As he flipped through, something about the title—The Culper Spy Ring—nagged at the back of his mind. He vaguely remembered hearing about it in history class, but this felt different, more personal. He skimmed a few paragraphs and his interest grew.

The Culper Spy Ring was one of America's first successful espionage organizations. George Washington himself had been involved, relying on a handful of ordinary citizens to pass along secret messages, helping to outwit the British during the Revolutionary War. The ring had played a huge role in turning the tide of the war, providing information that led to key victories, including one of the most crucial—the defeat of the British in Yorktown. Without the spy ring's intelligence, the war might have ended very differently.

Sean's eyes darted over the underlined letters again, a chill creeping up his spine. It was like something out of one of the action movies he and Deacon loved to watch, except this was real. He could imagine these spies, using secret codes and hidden messages to send vital information right under the enemy's nose. And here it was, right in front of him.

Wait a minute...

He leaned forward, staring at the letters. Whoever had underlined these didn't do it randomly. His pulse quickened. What if these underlined letters were part of a code?

Glancing back at the cryptogram on the desk, Sean's mind raced. This has to be it. The book is the key. He grabbed a pen and started matching the underlined letters to the cryptogram, his hand moving faster and faster as pieces began to fall into place.

Symbols began to form words, words began to form fragments of sentences. His heart pounded harder with each one. There was something ominous about the message, something that didn't sit right. His eyes widened as the meaning of the cryptogram became clear. It wasn't just some historical puzzle—it was a warning.

A warning of danger.

Sean's breath caught in his throat, and he shot up from the desk, knocking the chair over in his rush. "Deacon!" he called out, but there was no response. Deacon was already too far away, likely still outside on the phone.

His stomach twisted. He needed to tell Deacon, but before he could take another step, a loud, heavy knock echoed through the cabin, reverberating off the wooden walls. Sean froze, his pulse quickening.

The knock came again, harder this time, more insistent.

No, no, no. Sean rushed toward the front of the cabin, the cryptogram clutched in his hand. "Deacon!" he shouted again, rounding the corner just in time to see his best friend, oblivious, reaching for the door handle.

"Wait!" Sean's voice came out in a desperate yell, but it was too late. Deacon's hand was already on the knob, starting to turn.

The knock echoed one last time.

Chapter 4
A Knowledgeable Stranger

Deacon hesitated for just a second before pulling the door open. Standing on the porch was a man who instantly commanded attention—a tall, dark-haired figure with piercing green eyes that locked onto Deacon's with an intensity that reminded him of a panther he'd once seen at the zoo. The man's olive tanned skin and the way he held himself—fit but not overly muscular, like someone who was agile and used to moving with purpose—raised the hairs on the back of Deacon's neck, though he wasn't entirely sure why.

"Deacon Koster?" The man's voice was smooth but carried a weight to it, like someone who wasn't used to being questioned.

"Yeah, that's me," Deacon replied cautiously.

The man smiled, though it didn't quite reach his eyes. "I can see him in you. I'm Hugo Deroche. I was a friend of your uncle's—Cump."

Deacon's heart skipped a beat at the mention of his uncle. "You knew him?"

Hugo nodded, his green eyes softening just a touch. "Knew him well. Grew up with him and your dad. We were... quite the trio back in the day."

Deacon stepped aside to let Hugo in. As soon as the man crossed the threshold, Deacon noticed something—Hugo scanned the room in a way that felt too familiar. It was the same way Bob, his foster dad, always checked a room when they entered—casual, but thorough. Taking note of exits, potential dangers. It was a habit Bob said never really went away after his years in the SEALs. Now, seeing Hugo do the same thing, Deacon's gut tightened. Who was this guy really?

Deacon led Hugo to the living room, gesturing for him to sit. "So, you grew up with my uncle and my dad?"

Hugo sat down, crossing one leg over the other with a relaxed ease, though Deacon sensed a tension beneath the surface. "That's right. We were inseparable back in the day. Used to tear up the backwoods of Prince William County outside of D.C.. Your grandpa—bit of a history buff, to say the least—named your uncle and dad after two of the greatest friends in American military history, Generals Tecumseh Sherman and Ulysses S. Grant. Kind of ironic, considering what happened between them."

"What do you mean?" Deacon asked, leaning forward, eager for any scrap of information about his family.

"Well, Cump—your uncle Tecumseh—he was all about following in the family's footsteps. Our families, the Kosters and the Deroches, have followed a certain... path for generations. But your dad, Ulysses, wasn't as convinced." Hugo's smile was tight, his words intentionally vague, as though testing how much he should reveal.

Deacon frowned. "What kind of path?"

Hugo's gaze drifted to the window, choosing his words carefully. "A path of... service, you might say. One that's focused on helping people, protecting them in ways they might not even realize. Your uncle believed it was important work, but your dad—he wasn't sure he wanted to be tied to something like that. He had his own ideas about how to make a difference." Hugo paused, eyes flicking to Deacon's. "I see a lot of that in you, you know. The curiosity. The caution."

Deacon felt a jolt of something-pride, maybe? "So, what did my uncle actually do?"

Hugo leaned back slightly, his eyes flicking back to Deacon's. "Your uncle worked on projects that took him all over the world. He was dedicated, always going wherever he was needed. The last project he worked on was important, but he didn't get the chance to finish it before he died."

Deacon's heart thudded in his chest. "What kind of project?"

Hugo gave a faint smile, his voice growing softer. "It was something that involved helping people. Specific people, in different parts of the world. Think of it like... a charity, or a security group, helping where help was needed. The details are complicated, but your uncle was committed to it. I'd like to finish his last project but need something he was working on."

Deacon frowned. "What is it?"

Hugo smiled, though again, it didn't quite reach his eyes. "A box. It's small, nothing flashy. He stored it in a shed by the lake, tucked away like it was no big deal."

"A box?" Deacon's mind raced. "Why do you need it?"

"Let's just say it contains some important documents," Hugo replied casually, but there was something too casual about it, as if he was trying to downplay the significance. "Nothing dangerous, I promise. I just need to get it to finish my work."

Deacon's eyes narrowed slightly. Something about Hugo's tone felt off. It reminded him of a lesson one of his foster mothers, a detective, had taught him once: the more casual someone tries to make something seem, the more you should be suspicious. He had that same gut feeling now.

"Why was it stored in a shed?" Deacon asked, trying to push through the fog of half-truths Hugo was weaving.

Hugo waved a hand dismissively. "Cump didn't always go for the obvious spots. Sometimes, the best place to hide something is out in the open."

Deacon wasn't sure. If this box was so important, why would his uncle stash it somewhere so... random? His thoughts tangled as he tried to make sense of what Hugo was asking. Was he being too paranoid? It was just a box in a shed, after all. How dangerous could it really be?

But then, there was that feeling. That nagging suspicion that something wasn't right. He looked at Hugo, who was now sitting back in his chair, watching him with those sharp, panther-like eyes. The way Hugo scanned the room earlier. The subtle tension in his voice. It all felt calculated.

"Look, Deacon," Hugo said, his voice softening. "I get it—this is overwhelming. But your uncle trusted me, and I owe it to him to see this through."

Deacon stared at Hugo for a long moment, weighing his options. He could give Hugo the benefit of the doubt—he clearly knew a lot about Cump, more than Deacon had ever known about his uncle. But the little signs, the subtle shifts in Hugo's demeanor, were warning him to be cautious.

"So... can I go get the box?" Hugo asked, his tone light but with a hint of urgency creeping in.

Deacon glanced out the window toward the lake. The shed sat innocuously at the water's edge, just visible through the trees. It looked harmless enough.

He turned back to Hugo, unsure of what to say. Trust wasn't something Deacon gave easily, and this situation felt like it was spinning out of his control.

"I... I don't know," Deacon muttered. "I mean, I've just got here. I don't even know what's in that shed."

Hugo smiled again, his green eyes narrowing slightly. "I understand. Take your time, think about it. But don't take too long, okay? Some things... can't wait forever."

Deacon nodded, the weight of Hugo's words settling heavily on his shoulders. As Hugo stood to leave, Deacon's mind raced. Was this stranger really here to help? Or was there something far more dangerous at play?

As Hugo walked out the door, Deacon stood frozen, unsure whether he had just let in an ally or someone far more dangerous.

Chapter 5
Cryptic Warning

Deacon stood by the door, watching as Hugo gave him a tight-lipped smile. "Take your time thinking it over," Hugo said, but there was a flash of something in his green eyes—something that looked suspiciously like irritation. Deacon noticed the way Hugo's jaw clenched for just a second before he relaxed again.

"I will," Deacon replied cautiously, his hand still gripping the door. "I just need to settle in first. This is all... a lot." He hoped the excuse didn't sound too flimsy.

Hugo nodded, though it seemed like he was already growing impatient. "I understand. Just know I'm around if you have any questions about your uncle. Or if you change your mind about the box."

"Sure," Deacon said, forcing a smile. He watched as Hugo stepped off the porch and strode toward the driveway, disappearing into the growing shadows of the late afternoon.

Deacon shut the door behind him, releasing a breath he hadn't realized he was holding. Something about Hugo didn't sit right. That momentary flash of frustration—Deacon had seen it, even if Hugo tried to mask it. And the way he scanned the room like he was sizing up the place had made Deacon's skin crawl.

Just as he turned to head back into the living room, Sean rushed in, nearly colliding with him. "Dude! You will not believe what I just found."

Deacon raised an eyebrow. "What are you talking about?"

Sean was breathless, clutching a worn-out book in one hand. "Remember that cryptogram? I think I figured it out. Well, not me—this book." He held up the book titled The Culper Spy Ring. "There were letters underlined throughout it, like someone was leaving clues. It matches the cryptogram perfectly."

Deacon frowned, suddenly uneasy. "What do you mean, it matches?"

Sean pushed past him, heading toward the small office where they had found the cryptogram. "Look," he said, flipping open the book and pointing to the pages, his voice more urgent now. "I think the book was meant to help decrypt the message. And I've been working on it while you were talking to Hugo. It's a warning, Deacon. A serious one."

Deacon followed Sean into the room, his chest tightening as he glanced at the cryptogram now half-decoded on the desk. He could feel the intensity in Sean's words.

"A warning?" Deacon echoed, stepping closer. "From who?"

Sean glanced up at him, eyes wide. "It's a message to your uncle, I think. It says something like, 'The Order knows you have the key and has likely sent someone to retrieve it. You must protect it at all costs.'"

Deacon's heart pounded in his chest. "The Order? What... what does that even mean?"

"I have no idea," Sean admitted, flipping through the rest of the book as if answers would leap off the page. "But I don't think it's good news. And there's more—whoever wrote this knew that your uncle was being watched. It sounds like someone was after him. Maybe someone dangerous."

Deacon stared at the cryptogram, his mind racing. "So, you're saying my uncle was into... what, spy stuff? Like, some secret group was after him?"

Sean met Deacon's gaze, his face serious. "I don't know what the Order is, but if this cryptogram is right, then yeah. Your uncle was mixed up in something big. And dangerous. Which means that Hugo guy..." Sean trailed off, his expression darkening. "He's probably one of them."

Deacon's stomach turned. It all started to fall into place—the mysterious project, the way Hugo was so eager to get his hands on that box. And now, this cryptic message about an Order.

Deacon sat down heavily in the chair by the desk. "Hugo did seem... off. He got irritated when I told him I wasn't ready to help him yet."

"Exactly," Sean said, his voice rising. "He was in a rush for a reason, man! What if he's the one the Order sent to get that box? He could've been lying about being your uncle's friend."

Deacon shook his head slowly, trying to piece it all together. "I don't know, Sean. He knew a lot about Cump and my dad. But... I don't think I can trust him."

"We can't take any chances," Sean said, his tone urgent. "Whatever's in that box, it's clearly important. Your uncle died before he could finish whatever he was doing, and now someone's after it. Maybe Hugo's trying to cover up something your uncle left behind."

Deacon's mind reeled with possibilities. He had been so eager to learn more about his family, and now, this was what he had uncovered. His uncle was involved in something secretive and potentially dangerous, and now, he might be in the crosshairs too.

"What do we do?" Deacon asked, his voice barely above a whisper.

Sean's eyes were sharp. " No one touches that box until we know the truth. We have to get ahead of this—fast."

Deacon nodded slowly, his resolve hardening. "Okay. I'll tell Hugo he can't get the box. Not yet."

"Good," Sean said, relief in his voice. "But be careful, man. He's not who he says he is."

Deacon's mind raced as he stood up. The cryptogram, the warning about the Order, Hugo's irritation—it was all adding up. But he needed to be smart about this. Hugo might be lying, or worse, he might be a danger to them both.

As Deacon prepared to confront Hugo, one thing became clear: whatever was happening, his uncle had left him more than just an estate. He had left him a legacy of secrets and danger. And now, Deacon and Sean were caught in the middle of it.

Chapter 6
A Midnight Run

Deacon sighed, rolling onto his side and glancing out the window. The moon cast a pale light over the cabin grounds, and just as he was about to close his eyes, he noticed something moving. A shadow darted across the open ground behind the house, slipping into the woods where the trail to the lake started. Deacon squinted, his heart quickening.

It was Hugo.

But he wasn't just leaving. It had been hours since Hugo had left the cabin, and now, here he was, sneaking toward the lake in the dead of night. Something was up.

Deacon shot out of bed, adrenaline coursing through him. He quickly padded down the hall to Sean's room and knocked softly. "Sean, wake up."

Sean stirred, his voice groggy. "What is it, man?"

"Hugo's sneaking off to the lake. I just saw him."

That woke Sean up. He scrambled out of bed, grabbing his hoodie. "What? Where's he going?"

"I don't know," Deacon whispered, already pulling on his sneakers. "But we're gonna find out."

They hurried to get dressed, slipping quietly out the back door and into the cool night air. The forest surrounding the lake was dark, the moon barely filtering through the trees as they followed Hugo's trail. They stayed just far enough behind to avoid being seen, crouching low as they moved from shadow to shadow.

As they approached the lake, they saw Hugo slip inside the old boat shed, the door creaking faintly behind him.

Deacon glanced at Sean. "We need to get closer."

They crouched behind a thick tree, watching as Hugo disappeared into the shed. Deacon held his breath as they waited. Then, after a few tense seconds, they crept forward and crouched near the shed's side window, peeking in.

Inside, Hugo was moving quickly, scanning the shelves and

equipment before heading to a corner of the shed. He knelt down and fumbled with something hidden behind an old tarp.

Deacon squinted, watching as Hugo uncovered a secret door in the floor. He pulled it open, revealing a passageway that descended deep underground.

"Is that... a hidden tunnel?" Sean whispered, his eyes wide.

Deacon nodded. "Looks like it."

They watched as Hugo disappeared into the tunnel. Without wasting any time, the boys slipped into the shed, the scent of old wood and lake water thick in the air. Deacon hesitated at the open passageway, listening for any sounds from below. When all seemed clear, they carefully descended into the tunnel.

The passage was narrow and winding, the walls cold and damp. They could hear the faint sound of Hugo's footsteps echoing ahead, leading deeper into the earth. It felt like they were descending forever before the tunnel finally opened into a large underground cave.

Deacon motioned for Sean to hide behind a stack of crates at the edge of the room. From their hiding spot, they watched as Hugo made his way to the far side of the cave, where an old metal safe was embedded in the stone wall. Hugo knelt in front of it, unlocking the door with practiced precision.

Deacon's heart pounded as the safe swung open with a creak, revealing a small wooden box nestled among a pile of documents and artifacts.

"That's the box," Deacon murmured, his pulse quickening.

Before Hugo could take the box out, the sound of heavy footsteps echoed from the tunnel behind them. Deacon's stomach dropped as three large men entered the cave, their eyes locked on Hugo. They looked like trouble—broad-shouldered, clad in dark clothing, and with the same cold, focused demeanor that sent a shiver down Deacon's spine.

Hugo spun around, his eyes narrowing, but he didn't flinch. As two of the men advanced on him, Hugo was ready. He threw a punch, landing squarely on the first man's jaw, sending him stumbling back.

The third man, however, ignored the fight at first. His focus was on the safe—and the box.

Deacon and Sean watched, frozen, as the man approached the safe. "We have to stop him," Sean whispered urgently. But Deacon hesitated. They were outnumbered, and Hugo was already engaged in a fight.

The man opened the safe and reached for the box. Just as his fingers grazed it, he glanced back at his companions. Hugo was holding his own, throwing kicks and punches with surprising agility, but the two men were tough. The third thug's eyes narrowed as he realized his partners were struggling to subdue Hugo.

He left the box and rushed to help them.

Deacon's heart raced. This was their chance. He looked at Sean and gave a quick nod before darting out from behind the crates. He sprinted toward the safe, his pulse pounding in his ears. Without wasting a second, Deacon snatched the wooden box from the safe and stuffed it into his backpack.

Just as he secured the bag's zipper, Hugo was knocked to the ground with a heavy thud, his head hitting the stone floor. The fight stopped, and all three men turned toward Deacon.

Their eyes locked on the backpack slung over his shoulder.

"Hey!" one of them shouted, his voice echoing in the cave.

Deacon froze for a split second, dread flooding his veins. They knew. They knew he had the box.

The men advanced, their expressions dark with fury.

"Deacon, run!" Sean hissed, his voice sharp with urgency.

But Deacon barely moved. His heart hammered in his chest

as he realized there was nowhere to run. They were trapped. The tunnel behind them was the only exit, and the men were blocking their way.

The thugs closed in, their eyes fixed on Deacon and the precious box in his backpack.

They were out of time.

Chapter 7
Run!

Deacon's pulse pounded in his ears as the three men closed in. Sean's wide eyes darted around the cave, desperately searching for a way out.

"There!" Sean hissed, pointing to a barely visible passage off to the side, almost hidden by the shadows. The entrance was narrow and led slightly uphill.

Without thinking, Deacon nodded, and they bolted toward the passage. The sound of heavy footsteps and angry shouts echoed behind them as they sprinted into the dark tunnel.

"Where does this go?" Deacon asked, his breath ragged as they ran.

Sean shook his head, his voice breathless. "No clue, but do you really care? It's gotta be better than sticking around here!"

The passage was rough and winding, the stone walls slick with moisture. It twisted upward, making it hard to keep their footing. Behind them, the echoes of their pursuers grew louder.

Just when it felt like they couldn't go any farther, the tunnel opened up into a small barn-like structure. Pale light worked its way through cracks in the wooden walls. In the middle of the space, covered in a fine layer of dust, sat a lone ATV.

Deacon's heart leapt. "We're taking that."

Sean ran to the ATV, looking back toward the tunnel. The footsteps were getting closer. "You can drive this thing, right?"

"Yeah, kind of," Deacon replied, yanking off the dusty cover. He jumped on, his hands trembling as he checked the ignition. His heart sank. "Where are the keys?"

Sean groaned, frantically searching around the vehicle. "They've gotta be here somewhere!"

The pounding footsteps were almost at the tunnel's exit now. Deacon's stomach tightened. "Hurry up, man!"

Sean scanned the room in desperation, his eyes landing on the carved wooden support beam next to them. "There!" he shouted, pointing just above head-height at a small carving in the beam of an "all-seeing eye" symbol, just like the one on the dollar bill.

Dashing over to it, Sean pressed the carving. With a soft click, a hidden compartment slid open, revealing a set of keys.

He tossed them to Deacon just as the men's voices reached the entrance of the barn. "Go, go, go!"

Deacon jammed the keys into the ignition, his hands shaking. The engine roared to life, loud and angry in the small space. Sean leaped onto the back, clinging tightly to Deacon.

Without a second to spare, they sped out of the barn just as the thugs burst through the passageway. Dirt and gravel flew behind them as they tore through the trees, the shouts of the men fading into the distance.

Deacon gripped the handlebars hard, his mind racing. The ATV bounced over the rough terrain, the branches and underbrush whipping against them as they sped deeper into the woods. The pre-dawn light was just beginning to filter through the pines, casting long, eerie shadows across their path.

They didn't slow down. Deacon's heart was pounding, his mind spinning with questions and fear. But they were moving. They were getting away.

After several minutes, the terrain evened out, and Deacon slowed just a bit, his muscles aching from the tension.

"We made it!" Sean shouted over the roar of the engine, his voice equal parts relief and disbelief.

Deacon didn't respond. His mind was still in overdrive. They had escaped for now, but where could they go? And why was that box so important?

As they weaved through the trees, Deacon's thoughts kept circling back to one thing—who were those men, and why had they come after Hugo? He couldn't shake the feeling that this was bigger than anything they had imagined.

Just ahead, the trail opened up into a clearing. Deacon slowed even more, letting out a breath he didn't realize he'd been holding. "Maybe we lost them," he said, glancing back at Sean.

Sean gave a shaky nod, his grip on Deacon's shoulder relaxing. "Yeah. I think we're good."

For a moment, it seemed like they were in the clear. The woods were quiet, the pre-dawn light causing the dew to shimmer like a million tiny diamonds on the grass.

Then, in the distance, they heard it—a high pitched whine. Deacon's stomach dropped. "No way."

The whine grew louder, unmistakable now, separating into multiple distinct points.

Sean's eyes widened in panic. "Are those...dirt bikes?"

Deacon's heart raced again. "Oh no."

The noise grew closer, the unmistakable sound of engines revving, cutting through the stillness of the woods. Deacon twisted the throttle, the ATV roaring back to full speed.

"They're coming after us!" Sean shouted, gripping Deacon

tighter.

Deacon didn't need to be told twice. The chase wasn't over—it had just begun.

They sped into the trees once again, the sound of the dirt bikes closing in fast.

Chapter 8
Cliffside

Deacon pressed his back against the cool, jagged rock, his breath shallow as he glanced down at the wreckage of the ATV below. The twisted metal lay in a heap, half-buried by broken branches and dirt, where it had slammed into the ground after they'd driven it off the cliff.

Sean was next to him, gripping the edge of the rock face, his knuckles white. Above them, they could still hear the low hum of the single rider's dirt bike engine as he idled at the cliff's edge.

The rider hadn't seen them—at least not yet—but they had overheard his words.

"The Order won't let this slip through their fingers. They've already sent someone to deal with the traitor."

Deacon's heart was pounding as he replayed the words over and over in his head. The Order. Whoever these people were, they were organized, dangerous, and Hugo wasn't one of them.

The dirt bike rider revved his engine and sped off, the sound slowly fading as he drove back into the forest, likely regrouping with the other men.

Sean looked over at Deacon, his wide eyes filled with panic. "Did you hear that?"

Deacon nodded, his mind spinning. "He said 'The Order.' It's the same thing we read in the cryptogram. They're after the key, just like it said."

Sean swallowed hard. "And they called Hugo a traitor. He's not with them."

Deacon's chest tightened. The rider's words had shattered their earlier suspicions about Hugo. He wasn't the bad guy—he was in danger, just like they were.

"What if we were wrong about him?" Deacon said, glancing over the cliff one last time to make sure the coast was clear. "What if Hugo's been trying to protect us this whole time?"

Sean leaned back against the rock, his breath steadying as the realization sank in. "We've gotta go back, don't we? If The Order's after him, he's the only one who can help us figure out what to do next."

Deacon nodded, his heart still racing. "Yeah. He's the only one with answers.

They climbed back up from the cliff, careful to stay low and out of sight, and retraced their steps through the forest. By the time they reached the cave, the heat of the day had already settled in. They approached cautiously, but something was off. The cave was empty—no Hugo, no sign of a struggle, nothing.

"He's gone," Sean muttered, scanning the area. "What now?"

Deacon frowned, his mind turning over their options. "If he's not here, maybe he went back to the cabin."

Sean hesitated, then nodded. "Worth a shot."

The hike back to the cabin felt longer than it actually was, their steps weighed down by uncertainty. What if Hugo wasn't there? What if they were walking right into another trap? He wasn't just putting himself in danger—he was putting Sean at risk too. His heart tightened at the thought. If Sean got hurt because of him… No, he couldn't let that happen. But something about this felt different now. Deacon couldn't explain it, but his gut told him Hugo wasn't the enemy.

As they approached the cabin, Deacon slowed, eyes scanning the area. There, through the open window, he saw Hugo sitting on the couch. He was slumped over, nursing a lump on his head, with several cuts and bruises covering his face.

Deacon exchanged a glance with Sean, then cautiously pushed open the door. Hugo looked up, eyes bloodshot but sharp, as they entered.

"You're back," Hugo said hoarsely, a hint of relief mixed with surprise in his voice.

Deacon nodded, setting his backpack down. "We are. And we need answers."

Hugo winced as he shifted in his seat. "I bet you do. But first, can you... help with this?" He gestured to the cuts on his face.

Deacon blinked, surprised by the sudden shift, but nodded. "Yeah, I can help."

Deacon grabbed the first aid kit Judy had taught him to always keep around, his hands steadying as he started cleaning and dressing Hugo's wounds. Sean hovered nearby, watching cautiously but silently.

As Deacon worked, Hugo winced but didn't say anything at first. The tension in the room was thick—questions hanging in the air, waiting for answers. When Deacon finished, he sat back, his eyes locked on Hugo's.

"Tell us the truth," Deacon said quietly, his tone firm. "The whole truth."

Hugo studied both boys for a long moment, his eyes narrowing as if weighing his options. The silence stretched out, and Deacon could feel Sean shifting uncomfortably beside him.

Hugo exhaled slowly, his expression softening. "You two are more impressive than I thought."

Deacon frowned, taken aback. "What?"

Hugo leaned forward, ignoring the pain in his head. "You just eluded three highly trained men. Enemy agents. And you got away with something they've been after for a long time."

Sean shifted nervously. "So, what? Does that mean you're on our side?"

Hugo hesitated, then nodded slowly. "Yeah. I'm on your side. And your uncle's side. I've been trying to protect you... protect the key."

"The key?" Deacon repeated, glancing at the box.

Hugo glanced at the wooden box, then back at the boys. "There's a lot you don't know yet. And a lot I'm still not sure if I can tell you."

"Wait, wait, wait," Sean said, both hands in front of him in a halting gesture. "Can we rewind a minute to the part about ENEMY AGENTS?"

Deacon felt a surge of frustration. "Why not? You said you were on our side," ignoring his friend's interjection.

Hugo sighed, rubbing the back of his neck. "It's not that simple. But seeing you two out there... surviving... maybe you're more capable than I thought."

Deacon's frustration boiled over. "We've been chased, shot at, and we still don't know why! Now there's someone, or something called The Order that seems to be after us? If you're trying to protect us, then tell us what's going on!"

Hugo paused, the mention of his ancient rival momentarily catching him off guard. His brow furrowed with thought. The boys had proven themselves tonight, that much was clear. He had doubted whether they could handle the truth, but maybe... maybe they could.

"Alright," Hugo said, leaning back with a heavy sigh. "I'll tell you everything. But not yet."

Deacon scowled, but Sean placed a hand on his shoulder. "Okay. But we're gonna hold you to it."

Hugo gave a weak nod. "I expect you will. Rest for now. We're both going to need it. I'm afraid this is just getting started."

As Deacon sat back, he felt the weight of Hugo's words settling over him. He didn't know what the next step would be, but he knew one thing for certain—they weren't out of the woods yet. And whatever was coming next, it seemed the three of them would be facing it together.

Chapter 9
Guardians

Deacon stirred awake, his senses slowly adjusting to the soft, rhythmic sizzle of bacon. The cabin was filled with the smell of breakfast, and for a moment, he forgot where he was—halfway across the country, far from the life he had known just days ago. He blinked, rubbing the sleep from his eyes as he sat up.

Sean was already awake, propped up on his elbows in the room across the hall, his eyes fixed on the ceiling. "You smell that?" he asked groggily, sitting up.

Deacon nodded, pulling on a hoodie as he got out of bed. "Yeah. Hugo must be up."

They made their way out of the room and down the narrow hallway toward the kitchen, where they found Hugo standing at the stove, a spatula in hand and a smirk on his face.

"Morning," Hugo said, glancing back over his shoulder. "Figured you boys could use a real breakfast after the night we had."

Deacon struggled to contain a yawn. "I didn't realize you cooked *and* broke into other people's property."

Hugo flipped a piece of bacon expertly. "I learned from my mother. French women—very serious about their cooking." He placed the bacon on a plate already piled with eggs and toast and gestured for them to sit at the table. "Have a seat. We have a lot to talk about."

Deacon exchanged a glance with Sean before they both sat down. The events of the previous night still hung over them—the chase, the cryptogram, and the revelation that Hugo wasn't their enemy. But they had so many questions, and now it seemed they might finally get some answers.

Hugo set the plates in front of them and took a seat across the table. His usually guarded expression had softened just slightly, but there was still a seriousness in his eyes.

"My family... your family," Hugo began, his voice steady. "We are not like everyone else. We've spent centuries serving a higher purpose. Protecting the world from forces that most people can't even comprehend." He paused, watching their reactions. "For hundreds of years, the men and women in our families have been part of an organization called the Guardians."

Sean raised an eyebrow. "Guardians of what, exactly?"

"Of civilization," Hugo replied simply. "Of stability. Of order." He leaned forward slightly, his voice dropping. "There are forces in this world—ancient, powerful forces—that want to see it all come crashing down. The Guardians' job is to stop that from happening."

Deacon frowned, trying to wrap his head around it all. "So... like, what? You're some kind of secret society?"

Hugo chuckled softly. "I suppose you could call us that. But we're not just shadowy figures pulling strings from the sidelines. We're real people, with real lives, who have to make real decisions. And those decisions often decide the fate of nations, whether people realize it or not."

Sean, always skeptical, leaned back in his chair. "This sounds a little... far-fetched, man. No offense, but how does that explain the whole 'Order' thing?"

Hugo's face darkened slightly at the mention of the Order. "The Order is our enemy. They're just as old as we are, maybe older. But where we seek to maintain stability and protect humanity, they seek chaos and control. Their goal is to disrupt the world—to tear it apart from the inside, so they can rebuild it in their image."

Deacon's brow furrowed as he considered Hugo's words. "But why? What's in it for them?"

"Power," Hugo said, his voice grim. "Wealth. Influence. The Order doesn't care about the well-being of the world, only about how they can bend it to their will. And they're very good at what they do."

Sean leaned forward again, his curiosity piqued. "So, you're like the good guys, and they're the bad guys? Angels and demons kind of thing?"

Hugo shook his head. "No. We're just people, same as them. But we've been fighting this battle for centuries. Sometimes we win, sometimes we don't. But it's never-ending."

Deacon's mind was spinning. "Why don't you just go to the government? Get them to help you take out the Order?"

Hugo smiled, but there was a sadness in his eyes. "It's not that simple, Deacon. There are rules—strict rules. Guardians and Order members aren't supposed to take direct action against each other under normal circumstances. If I knew an Order operative was sitting right in front of me, I couldn't attack them without risking a greater conflict. But... those rules get bent when personal vendettas come into play, or when both sides are after something they deem crucial enough. And we absolutely can't expose each other to civilians. That would cause chaos, and that's exactly what the Order wants."

Sean scoffed. "So, what do you do? Sit back and hope they don't destroy the world?"

"Not quite," Hugo replied, his tone becoming more serious. "We use influence. We nudge things in the right direction. We make it so people and organizations end up doing what we want them to do, without ever knowing we're involved. That's how we fight."

Deacon shook his head, still struggling to process everything. "So... all this time, my uncle was part of this? And now I'm supposed to just... what? Join up?"

Hugo's gaze softened. "Your uncle was one of the best operatives we had. And you, Deacon—you come from one of the most distinguished Guardian families. The Kosters. It's in your blood."

Deacon stared down at his plate, feeling the weight of Hugo's words settle on him. "What about the box?" he asked quietly, pulling the small wooden box out of his backpack and setting it on the table. "What does this have to do with all of this?"

Hugo's eyes locked onto the box, and for the first time since they'd met, Deacon saw a flicker of real emotion cross Hugo's face—something between awe and fear.

"That," Hugo said softly, "is a key. A key to something that could change everything."

Deacon glanced at Sean, who looked just as confused as he felt. "What kind of key?"

Hugo leaned back in his chair, his gaze never leaving the box. "That, my friend, is an interesting story indeed."

Chapter 10
The Spy's Gambit

August 1780 - New York City

The flickering candlelight cast long shadows on the brick walls of the small basement beneath Samuel Fraunces' coffee shop. The smell of strong coffee mixed with the dampness of the underground room. Agent 732, Robert Townsend, leaned over his wooden desk, hurriedly scratching ink onto parchment. Every stroke of the quill felt like a race against time, the urgency of the moment pressing on his shoulders like a vice.

The room was quiet, save for the soft scratching of quill on paper, but Townsend knew the stillness was an illusion. Above ground, the bustling streets of British-occupied New York carried on as if nothing was amiss. But in the shadows, unseen eyes hunted him.

Townsend wasn't just carrying information that could alter the course of the Revolutionary War—he was in possession of something far more dangerous. His hand drifted to the small pouch inside his coat, where a smooth, cold object rested. The talisman. He could feel its presence, almost as if it had a life of its own, pulsing with ancient power.

He had never believed in magic, but after seeing what the

talisman could do, he wasn't sure what to believe anymore. He had used it only once, in a desperate moment, when his cover as a loyalist merchant was nearly blown. With the talisman in hand, he had made the British officer think he was someone else entirely—another trusted officer in the King's army. The deception had been perfect, seamless. And it was then he realized the true nature of the object he held: it wasn't mere trickery, but something far more profound, a kind of chemical reaction that altered the minds of those around him, making them malleable to his will.

But now, the talisman had become a double-edged sword. The shadowy figures pursuing him—agents of the Order, he suspected—wanted the talisman as much as the intelligence he carried. They knew of its power, perhaps even more than he did. He couldn't allow it to fall into their hands.

Time was running out. Townsend leaned back from the desk, surveying the map he had just finished drawing. It was no ordinary map. Hidden within its lines, symbols, and coordinates were layers of encoded information, designed to be deciphered only by a specially crafted ocular device he had commissioned months earlier—a device he hoped would help hide messages in plain sight. The map would lead the rightful bearer to the talisman's location, but only if they had the means to decode it.

He wrapped the map tightly with the intelligence report— the vital information he had painstakingly gathered about British troop movements and secret plans to block the French landings in Long Island. He sealed it with wax, imprinting it with his personal signet ring, and placed it into a leather pouch. This would go directly into the hands of General Washington through the Culper Ring's clandestine courier network.

A soft knock at the door startled him. Townsend quickly shoved the map into his coat pocket, rising to his feet. The knock came again, more insistent this time. He reached for the pistol on the desk, gripping it tightly.

"Who's there?" Townsend asked, his voice low and controlled.

"It's Caleb, sir," came the whispered reply from the other side of the door. The familiar voice of his nephew brought a flood of relief. Caleb Brewster was not just a nephew but a trusted courier and fellow spy in the Culper Ring. If anyone could be trusted with the talisman, it was him.

Townsend moved quickly, opening the door just enough to let Caleb slip inside. The young man was covered in the grime of travel, his face tense with urgency.

"Uncle, we don't have much time," Caleb whispered, glancing over his shoulder as though expecting someone to be lurking in the shadows. "They're closing in on you."

"I know," Townsend replied, his voice tight. "They want what I have. The intelligence... and this." He pulled the small pouch from his coat and handed it to Caleb. "You must take this. It's more than just a trinket—it's dangerous. Take it to the place we discussed and hide it so no one can find it. The map I'm sending to my friend in General Washington's camp will get it in the right hands eventually."

Caleb's eyes widened as he weighed the pouch in his hand. "What is it, Uncle?"

"Something beyond your understanding, and that of most men," Townsend said gravely. "It has the power to change minds, to alter reality itself. If the British—or worse—get their hands on it, we could lose everything."

Caleb nodded, slipping the pouch into his satchel. "I'll make sure it's safe. But you need to get out of here. They're not far behind."

"I'll delay them," Townsend said, his mind already working out the plan. "Go, now. Get to the docks. There's a ship bound for the West Indies. You'll sail with it. Once you're away, follow the instructions I've given you."

Caleb hesitated, concern etched across his features. "What about you?"

"I'll manage," Townsend said with a tight smile. "I always do."

Caleb gave a quick nod, then slipped out of the basement, leaving Townsend alone once more.

Townsend gathered his things quickly, his heart pounding as the sense of impending danger grew stronger. He extinguished the candle and moved toward the back exit of the basement, but before he could reach the door, the distant sound of boots echoed down the alley. The Order's agents were closing in.

No time.

He had only one chance to escape with his life—and the

precious intelligence that could change the course of the war.

Townsend hurried back to the desk, his pulse racing. He grabbed the remaining papers, shoving them into his coat. Then, with one last glance at the room, he slipped out the back door, disappearing into the maze of New York's narrow streets and alleys.

Just moments later, the door to the coffee shop burst open. Three men, clad in dark cloaks, stepped into the basement. Their eyes scanned the room, their movements precise and deliberate.

"He was here," one of them hissed, running a gloved hand over the desk. "But we're too late."

The leader of the group, his face hidden beneath the hood of his cloak, stared at the empty room with cold fury. "Find the traitor. And bring back the talisman. We cannot let it slip through our grasp again."

The men moved swiftly, disappearing back into the night, their pursuit relentless.

But Townsend was already gone, vanishing into the shadows with the knowledge that he had set in motion a plan that would keep the talisman—and the future of the revolution—out of the Order's hands.

For now.

Chapter 11
A Map Unfolds

Present

Deacon sat quietly at the kitchen table, staring at the weathered map in front of him. Hugo's voice echoed in his mind, recounting the events that had started this whole chain of mystery. Townsend had drawn the map with the intention of getting it into the hands of his Guardian contact in General Washington's camp, but fate had other plans. The map had ended up in Washington's personal papers, untouched for centuries until they were sold at auction. Somewhere along the way, Uncle Cump had acquired it and now, it sat before him. Living history staring up from yellowed paper.

Hugo pulled a worn leather-bound journal from his pack and held it up. The cover was cracked with age, the corners soft and frayed, but Deacon recognized it immediately from the attic—the journal they had found tucked away among Uncle Cump's belongings.

"This," Hugo said, "is where your uncle documented everything he discovered about the talisman, the Order, and its supposed origin." He flipped open the journal, revealing pages filled with Uncle Cump's neat, hurried handwriting.

Deacon leaned in, his curiosity piqued.

"Not much is known about the talisman itself," Hugo explained. "But Cump found some interesting pieces of the puzzle. According to his research, the talisman—or Pendant, as we believe it to be—was brought from Africa to the West Indies centuries ago. Some stories say it came from the Yoruba region, where a powerful stone was believed to have mystical properties. Cump suspected that the pendant wasn't magical in the way people thought, but rather that it contained a chemical compound that could influence the minds of those around it."

Sean frowned. "Chemical compound? Like some kind of hallucinogen?"

Hugo nodded. "Something like that. But here, let me read you one of the entries." He thumbed through the journal until he found the page he wanted.

August 15th

"After weeks of digging through old texts, I've come across several references to a pendant said to possess 'otherworldly power.' It appears that during the 18th century, a Yoruba priest was captured and enslaved, his belongings—including the pendant—confiscated. Some claim it could 'control the will of men,' though I suspect there's a scientific explanation. Perhaps it was a plant-based compound stored within the stone, something that could temporarily alter a person's mental state."

Deacon felt a chill run down his spine as he listened. His uncle had known more than Deacon realized, and it seemed the pendant was more dangerous than he had imagined.

Hugo continued. "Cump wasn't just investigating the history of the pendant. He also found evidence that the Order had been looking for it for centuries. In fact, the journal mentions exactly who has been tasked with its recovery."

He turned to another page and began to read:

September 4th

"The Order's reach extends deeper than even I thought. Its importance to their plans must have recently increased because Von Heger has now been mobilized to recover the talisman. I have no doubt that he wants more than just the talisman. I haven't faced Von Heger since Vienna three years ago, but I know what he's capable of. He's ruthless, methodical, and he clearly has a personal vendetta against our family."

Deacon's stomach tightened as he read the words. He could almost feel the weight of Cump's fear and the looming threat of Von Heger hanging over him. This wasn't just a faceless enemy—this was personal.

"Wait," Sean interrupted, "what does this guy have against your uncle?"

Hugo's expression darkened. "The grudge wasn't just against Tecumseh. The Von Heger family is old and powerful within the Order. They are kind of the Order's version of your family, Deacon."

Deacon swallowed hard. "So… this Von Heger family, they're like our family's rivals in this whole thing?"

Hugo's eyes were hard, his voice low. "The Von Hegers and Kosters have fought each other for centuries. If you're a Koster, you've got enemies in the Order, and the Von Hegers are at the top of that list. Your uncle knew that. He was careful not to drag you into this until you were ready, but Von Heger doesn't play by the same rules. The last major showdown between your two families was nearly 50 years ago and it did not end well for them. Von Heger's not just after the talisman; he's after revenge."

Deacon clenched his fists, a knot of anger forming in his

chest. The idea that this Von Heger might have been responsible for his uncle's death made everything feel even more personal. It wasn't just about stopping the Order from getting the talisman anymore—it was about making sure they didn't get away with what they'd done to his family.

Hugo continued flipping through the journal, pausing on an entry that seemed less significant than the others, but still caught his attention. "This entry is odd. It doesn't fit with the others, but it stood out to Cump."

September 18th
"In reviewing Townsend's old papers on colonial trade, I came across a reference to a place called Dead Man's Point. It's mentioned as an important stop in the smuggling routes used by merchants like him to avoid British tariffs. It struck me as odd. Why would Townsend care to mention an obscure, forgotten place like Dead Man's Point unless it held some significance?"

Deacon blinked, his brow furrowing. "Dead Man's Point?"

Hugo shrugged. "It didn't seem relevant to Cump at the time, but he made a note of it. It could mean something, or it could just be Townsend making a note of the best way to evade British taxes."

Sean leaned back; arms crossed. "Maybe it is. Or maybe there's more to it."

Hugo nodded. "Maybe. But we'll keep it in mind. If there's anything I've learned from Cump's research, it's that no detail is too small."

As Hugo closed the journal, Deacon sat back, digesting everything they'd just learned. The talisman—this mysterious pendant—was more dangerous than he had imagined, and now they knew for sure the Order had sent someone after it. Not just someone—Von Heger. And though Dead Man's Point didn't seem to matter now, Deacon couldn't shake the feeling that it might turn out to be important later.

"If they can reproduce the talisman's chemical…" Deacon muttered, his voice trailing off.

Hugo gave a solemn nod. "They'd be unstoppable. World leaders, powerful organizations, no one would be safe from their influence. That's why this has to be stopped."

The room was quiet, save for the ticking of the clock on the wall. Sean stood nearby, pacing in short bursts, clearly trying to wrap his mind around everything.

"So, where does the map lead?" Sean asked, breaking the silence.

Hugo leaned back in his chair, exhaling slowly. "We don't know yet. The Guardians never got the chance to follow it through. Cump had just acquired the key only the day before he…" Hugo's voice betrayed a catch, a slight loss of composure he hadn't shown before. "Before it became yours."

Sean glanced at Deacon, the excitement in his wide eyes warring with the obvious hurt Hugo was feeling. "You ready to finish what your Uncle started? Ready to break out the key and see where it leads?" he asked, his voice charged with anticipation.

Deacon looked at the map, then at the box sitting beside it on the table. His heart was pounding. So much had changed in just a few days, and now it felt like they were standing on the edge of something bigger than they could have ever imagined.

"Yeah," Deacon said, nodding slowly. "I'm ready." But instead of opening the box himself, he handed it to Sean. "You do it. You've got the knack for puzzles."

Sean's eyes lit up. He took the box eagerly, carefully lifting the lid to reveal the ocular device inside. It was a beautiful object—crafted from polished brown leather, shiny brass, and perfectly cut crystal lenses. The five legs on the bottom sat perfectly on the map, and the view port on the top gleamed in the light.

"Whoa," Sean whispered, clearly in awe of the device. He placed it gently on the map, aligning it with the markings.

Deacon watched as Sean twisted the top, his brow furrowed in concentration. Slowly, the random lines and markings on the map began to shift, aligning into a coherent pattern.

"I think it's coming together," Sean said, his voice barely above a whisper. He kept turning the ocular device, adjusting the focus until suddenly, everything snapped into place.

Deacon leaned in, staring through the viewport. There, clear as day, were latitude and longitude lines, along with a series of numbers.

Sean grabbed a notepad and scribbled them down quickly. "Coordinates," he said, grinning. Pulling out his smartphone, he typed in the digits and held it up for the other two to see. "For the northern coast of Jamaica."

"Jamaica?" Deacon repeated, his mind racing. This was really happening. They were uncovering something huge, something hidden for centuries.

But then Deacon's eyes fell on the numbers. "What about these?" he asked, pointing to the cryptic sequence that followed the coordinates.

Sean squinted at the numbers. "Another cryptogram," he said with a sigh. "But one thing at a time. We know where the map leads now. I'll see if I can see a pattern in them but without a key to work from, it's going to be tough."

Deacon sat back, feeling the weight of the decision in front of him. Jamaica wasn't just down the street. If they were going to follow this, they'd be committing to something much bigger.

They'd be diving headfirst into a world they barely understood. He barely had his driver's license, now he was supposed to jet off to some Caribbean island to stop an ancient evil secret society from taking over the world?

Hugo, sensing Deacon's hesitation, spoke up. "You've done more than enough already. I can take it from here. This is getting dangerous."

But Deacon shook his head. He had been dragged into this, sure, but now he was starting to feel a pull—a sense of obligation. If the Order got their hands on the talisman, the consequences would be catastrophic. Maybe it was the centuries of family service, or maybe it was just putting into practice what someone very brave once told him about facing an impossible situation – *'I Do What I Can'*.

"I can't just walk away from this," Deacon said, his voice firm. "I'm not ready to join the Guardians, but I'm not going to stand by and do nothing."

Hugo studied Deacon for a long moment, then nodded. "All right. But know this—once you're in, there's no going back. The Order won't stop. They'll come after you, after Sean. They won't rest until they have what they want."

Deacon exchanged a glance with Sean. "Looks like we're going to Jamaica."

Sean grinned. "Great, I've been looking for a reason to break out my new swim trunks."

Hugo stood, placing a hand on Deacon's shoulder. "Then get ready. This ride's about to start and there's no getting off until the end. Let's go find us a treasure."

Chapter 12
The Huntsman

Bavaria, Germany—The Von Heger Ancestral Castle

The study was a relic of old Europe, opulent and dark, lined with towering bookshelves crammed with ancient tomes and rare artifacts. The dim light of a flickering fire threw long shadows across the room, dancing off the polished wood paneling and the heavy velvet curtains drawn tight over tall, narrow windows. The air smelled faintly of cedar, leather, and the distinct scent of time, heavy with the weight of centuries of secrets.

At the center of it all sat Heinrich Von Heger.

He leaned back in a high-backed leather chair behind a grand mahogany desk, the surface covered with papers, maps, and a few carefully placed relics. His cold blue eyes flickered with an intelligence that was as piercing as it was unsettling. His dark hair was speckled with silver at the temples, neatly combed, though his pale face carried the worn lines of a man who had seen and orchestrated far too much.

The firelight glinted off a small crest pinned to his black vest—a stag, the ancient symbol of the Von Heger family, who had served the Order for generations. Heinrich had spent his entire life carrying the weight of their legacy, and now he was its master.

A faint vibration disturbed the air, emanating from a sleek, modern phone lying on his desk. It seemed out of place in a room so steeped in tradition, but Von Heger had always believed in wielding both old and new tools to serve his purposes.

He reached for the phone, not hurried but deliberate. There were few people who dared call him directly.

A voice crackled through the line as soon as he accepted the call. "Herr Von Heger, this is Castor. I regret to inform you that we were unable to secure the key from the Guardian's estate in North Carolina."

For a moment, there was only the crackling of the fire in the hearth as Von Heger processed the failure. He didn't speak, letting the silence weigh heavily on the caller. Castor's voice wavered slightly when he continued.

"The situation… became more complicated. The Guardian's nephew, Tecumseh Koster's nephew, Deacon, has somehow involved himself. He was there, along with one of his friends. It seems the boy may be in possession of the key now."

Von Heger leaned forward slightly, resting his elbows on the desk, his long fingers steepling in front of him. His face remained impassive, but the intensity in his gaze sharpened. Deacon Koster. So, Tecumseh's legacy lived on in that boy after all.

"I expected the Kosters to be resilient," Von Heger said, his voice low, almost a whisper. "But the nephew? Interesting. And this friend? Tell me more."

"His name is Sean, we think," Castor replied quickly. "We have no intel on him yet. But there was another man as well—Hugo. One of the Guardians, I believe."

Von Heger's lips twitched, a flicker of amusement crossing

his face. "Deroche. Of course. The Guardians would never leave a Koster unattended. Especially one so... young." He paused, the wheels of his mind already spinning. "And the map?"

"We believe they have it," Castor answered. "We were unable to locate it at the property, and they left before we could intercept them."

Von Heger stood slowly, walking to the tall, narrow window behind his desk. He pulled aside the heavy velvet curtain with one hand and looked out across the dark Bavarian countryside. The moonlight bathed the rolling hills in a pale glow, casting long, jagged shadows from the ancient trees surrounding the castle.

"They'll follow the map," Von Heger murmured, more to himself than to the man on the other end of the line. "That much is certain. It's in their nature to chase down what their ancestors protected. Tecumseh's nephew will feel compelled to complete the task his uncle started. It's predictable, really. They're always too sentimental."

He let the curtain fall back into place and turned toward the fire, watching the flames dance. His face remained calm, though his mind was already steps ahead of the Kosters.

"Here's what you will do," Von Heger said, his voice cutting through the silence like a blade. "Activate our informants. Every point of contact—airports, seaports, any travel network that could lead us to them. I want to know when they make a move. And when they do, you will follow them."

Castor hesitated for a moment. "Follow them, sir?"

"Yes." Von Heger's lips curled into a thin smile, though there was no warmth behind it. "Let them find what they're looking for. They've already gone further than most in uncovering Townsend's map and deciphering its secrets. We'll let them do the hard work." He paused, his voice hardening. "And then make sure they never leave."

A long silence followed as Castor absorbed the instructions. "Understood, Herr Von Heger. We'll be ready."

"One more thing," Von Heger added, his tone almost casual. "I want eyes on all of them. The boy, his friend, and Deroche. The Guardians are not to be underestimated. I will not accept failure twice."

"Yes, sir."

Von Heger ended the call and returned the phone to the desk, placing it down as if weightless. His eyes drifted to a glass case on the wall—inside, a dagger with an intricately carved hilt sat on display. A relic of a time when the world was governed by different rules, a time when his ancestors fought the Kosters with steel instead of shadows. But the game had changed. The pieces were still in motion, but now the battlefield was different.

He stepped closer to the case, staring at the dagger. "It's almost time," he whispered, his reflection in the glass warped and flickering with the firelight.

The Kosters thought they could outrun their past, that they could protect what the Guardians had hidden for centuries. But Von Heger knew better. The talisman would be his, and with it, he would ensure that the Von Heger legacy endured.

Turning away from the dagger, he walked slowly back to his desk, his mind already shifting toward the next move in this ancient game. Soon, the Kosters would realize they were not the hunters.

They were the prey—and Von Heger never missed his mark.

Chapter 13
No Man An Island

Montego Bay, Jamaica

The rumble of the airplane's landing gear jolted Deacon from his thoughts. They were finally here—Jamaica. The sunlit runway of Sangster International Airport stretched out below as the plane descended. Deacon glanced over at Sean, who was glued to his phone screen, scrolling furiously.

"No luck yet?" Deacon asked.

Sean shook his head, not looking up. "I've tried everything. There's no mention of any place called 'Thache's Grotto' anywhere. No tourist spots, no historical landmarks. It's like it doesn't exist."

It had only taken Sean a day to crack the map's cryptogram, but the message it contained was proving a bit harder to decipher.

Hugo, sitting in the aisle seat, leaned in. "It probably doesn't—not by that name, anyway. But we'll find it. We've got more resources to tap into once we're on the ground."

The plane touched down with a bump, and Deacon's stomach did a little flip—not just from the landing, but from the weight of everything ahead of them. Jamaica was beautiful, sure, but this wasn't a vacation. They were here to find something powerful, something dangerous. And so far, they were chasing shadows.

Once they cleared customs, Hugo rented a Jeep, the kind with open sides, perfect for navigating the uneven terrain they were likely to face. The midday sun was relentless, casting a golden glow over the island as they left the airport behind.

Sean still hadn't given up. "So, if this 'Thache's Grotto' isn't on any official records, what now? Where do we even start?"

Hugo navigated the winding road out of Montego Bay, his brow furrowed in thought. "We'll start with the basics—research. There's a cultural center nearby. They keep historical records that might not have made it into the online databases. That's probably our best shot."

The Montego Bay Cultural Centre wasn't far, nestled in the heart of the town, away from the bustling tourist areas. The building itself was a well-preserved colonial structure, its light gray stone walls cool against the tropical heat. Inside, the smell of old books and dust filled the air, a comforting contrast to the chaos outside.

Deacon and Sean followed Hugo through the entrance, their eyes scanning the room. It wasn't crowded, just a few researchers poring over old texts, the occasional tourist drifting through, more interested in the architecture of the old Georgian courthouse than the knowledge held within.

"Let's split up," Hugo suggested. "Start with anything from the 18th century. We're looking for references to place names that may have changed or disappeared over time. Anything that would have been well known to shipping merchants during that time."

Deacon nodded, and they set off through the maze of shelves. Rows of old books and manuscripts towered above them, and Deacon couldn't shake the feeling that the weight of history pressed down on them here—like they were surrounded by echoes of the past.

They searched for over an hour, skimming through records of old pirate activities, naval skirmishes, and colonial trade routes. But there was nothing—no mention of Thache's Grotto.

"I got nothing," Sean muttered, leaning against one of the shelves. "How does a place this important just not exist?"

"That's the point," Hugo said, his voice low as he approached. "If it was easy to find, we wouldn't need to be here."

Just as they were about to call it quits, a voice interrupted them.

"Excuse me, but I couldn't help overhearing. You're looking for something called 'Thache's Grotto,' right?"

Deacon turned to see a girl about his age standing a few feet away. She had olive skin, dark black hair pulled into a loose braid, and inquisitive hazel eyes. She was holding an old book in her hands, and her expression was a mix of curiosity and caution.

Sean blinked. "Uh, yeah. How'd you know?"

She shrugged, stepping a little closer. "I like to hang out here sometimes—just to be surrounded by all this history, you know? Anyway, I overheard you talking about some place from the 1700's that might be called something else now. My parents are professors on the island, and I help them with research sometimes. There's a small museum in town—the Bay Colonial Archives Museum. It's not big and a bit off the beaten path, but it specializes in 18th-century history, especially the colonial period here in Montego Bay. If anyone has heard of a place called Thache's Grotto, it'd be them."

Deacon exchanged a glance with Sean and Hugo. The museum sounded promising, but something about the timing felt... off. They had been searching for hours, and just as they were about to give up, someone conveniently showed up with the perfect lead?

"What's your name?" Deacon asked, trying to sound casual.

"Maria Cortez," she said. "I live here in Montego Bay. I'm kind of a history nerd. That museum is a bit of a hidden gem. Not a lot of tourists know about it."

Deacon nodded, but he felt a prickle of unease at the back of his neck. Hugo's eyes flickered, catching the same vibe.

"You sure this museum will have what we're looking for?" Hugo asked, his tone neutral but probing.

Maria hesitated, just for a second, then nodded. "Yeah. I mean, it's worth a shot, right?"

As they made their way out of the cultural center, Deacon couldn't shake the feeling that they were being watched. The air felt heavy, like someone was following their every move.

Just as they were leaving, he caught a glimpse of movement out of the corner of his eye—a shadowy figure slipping through the rows of bookshelves. It was quick, almost too quick, but enough to make Deacon's heart race.

He looked over at Hugo, who had stopped dead in his tracks, his eyes narrowed in the same direction.

"Did you see that?" Deacon whispered.

Hugo nodded, his hand drifting to his side, where Deacon knew he had a concealed knife.

"Come on," Hugo said, his voice barely above a murmur. "We should go."

As they stepped out into the bright sunlight, Sean glanced back inside, watching Maria slip deeper into the rows of shelves. She disappeared from view, and Deacon couldn't shake the unease settling in his gut.

"Think we can trust her?" Deacon asked, keeping his voice low.

Sean glanced at the entrance to the center, then shrugged. "She seems legit, but this whole thing does feel a little… convenient."

Hugo stood between them, his face unreadable. "It's possible we're being paranoid," he said. "But after everything we've seen so far, better to be cautious."

Deacon nodded, the weight of the situation pressing on him. He didn't know if Maria was leading them into a trap or if she genuinely wanted to help, but at this point they didn't have much choice.

"Let's check out the museum," Deacon said, his voice steady but cautious. "But stay sharp."

They walked into the bustling streets of Montego Bay, the sun beating down on them. As they made their way to the rented Jeep, Deacon couldn't help but glance over his shoulder every few minutes, half-expecting to see the shadowy figure from the library following them.

Whether it was paranoia or something else, the chase had begun.

Chapter 14
The Museum

The streets of Montego Bay were quieter than Deacon expected. The bustling energy of the airport had given way to narrow, almost forgotten alleys on the outskirts of the city. He, Sean, and Hugo now stood outside the Bay Colonial Archives Museum. It was a two-story colonial-style house, its age visible in the faded sky-blue paint and creaky shutters, but it felt like a relic from another time. Tucked away from the busy tourist attractions, it had an air of mystery, the kind of place that seemed to hold secrets waiting to be uncovered.

Hugo led the way inside, and Deacon immediately felt the change in atmosphere. The museum smelled of old paper and polished wood, and the walls were lined with books, artifacts, and paintings from Jamaica's colonial past. Light streamed through large windows, casting long shadows over the small but well-maintained collection.

They were greeted by a small, smiling woman who looked to be in her 60s. Her chocolate skin contrasted against the brilliant white of her teeth, and her demeanor was warm and inviting. "Welcome to the Bay Colonial Archives," she said, her voice a rich blend of Jamaican cadence and scholarly confidence. "I'm Dr. Jada Williams, curator of this little corner of history."

Hugo stepped forward. "We're hoping you can help us with something from the 18th century," he said. "We're looking for a place called Thache's Grotto."

Dr. Williams frowned slightly, her brow furrowing in thought. "Thache's Grotto?" She tapped her chin for a moment before her eyes lit up. "You mean Teach's Cave, perhaps? Edward Teach, or Blackbeard as he's more commonly known today, was said to have hidden in a small sea cave on the northern part of the island during his early pirate days. It's one of those local legends that's persisted. Although how true it is, I'm not sure we can say."

Deacon exchanged a glance with Sean. Teach's Cave—that had to be it.

"Do you know if there are any historical connections between the cave and a man named Caleb Brewster?" Sean asked, the excitement creeping into his voice.

Dr. Williams' eyes widened, recognition clear on her face. "Caleb Brewster. Now, that's a name I haven't heard in some time. Follow me."

She led them through a narrow hallway and down a small stairway into a lower level of the museum. There, among the various paintings and artifacts from the late 1700s, she stopped in front of a small oil painting. It depicted a young man, dressed in fine clothes of the time, standing near a cliff overlooking the ocean. Around his neck, glinting faintly in the painting's dim light, was a stone pendant.

"This is Caleb Brewster," Dr. Williams explained. "Quite the intriguing character. He was a successful merchant here in Jamaica for several years, though not many remember his name now. He disappeared mysteriously, and his story was all but forgotten. Rumor has it that he owned a house near Teach's Cave and was seen to walk up and down the shore at night. So, when he vanished, people swore they continued seeing someone walking there and it only added fuel to the legends about that place being haunted."

Deacon stared at the painting, the pendant catching his attention immediately. That had to be the talisman. Brewster hadn't hidden it like he was supposed to.

"What happened to him?" Deacon asked, trying to keep the growing urgency out of his voice.

Dr. Williams shook her head. "No one knows for sure. But stories about the cave being haunted persisted for years after he disappeared."

She pulled out her phone and began typing. After a moment, she pulled out a pen and began writing. Smiling, she handed Deacon a small slip of paper. "Here are the coordinates to Teach's Cave. It's not a popular tourist spot, and there are no paved roads going directly there, but you should be able to find it easily enough with these."

Deacon took the paper, his heart racing. "Thank you, Dr. Williams," Hugo said, offering a polite nod.

As they left the museum, the sun had dipped lower in the sky, casting long shadows in the alley. Deacon was about to suggest they head for the Jeep when a sudden movement caught his eye.

Out of nowhere, two men lunged from the alleyway, their faces twisted with determination. Order agents.

"Get down!" Hugo shouted as he shoved Deacon aside, dropping to a fighting stance.

One of the agents charged at Hugo, fists swinging, but Hugo blocked the attack and countered with swift precision. The agent stumbled back, momentarily disoriented.

The second agent, however, had his sights set on Sean and Deacon. He was closing in fast, his hand outstretched, ready to snatch the coordinates from Deacon's hand.

Deacon's heart raced. They were trapped.

Just as the agent was about to grab him, a figure darted out from behind a stack of crates. Maria.

She slammed into the agent with surprising force, shoulder first, sending him crashing to the ground. "Come on!" she shouted. "We don't have much time!"

For a split second, both agents were down, but Deacon knew they wouldn't stay that way for long. He glanced at Hugo, who had already subdued his attacker and was looking for something to use as rope to tie him up.

"Follow me!" Maria called, her eyes wide with urgency. "I know somewhere safe. Trust me."

Deacon hesitated. Could they trust her? This could all be part of an elaborate trap, but what choice did they have? He looked at Sean, whose expression mirrored his uncertainty.

Hugo hopped up and ran over to them, his eyes raised questioningly. The two Order agents began to get to their feet as well. Deacon had to make a decision. But would it be the right one, or were they just moving from one danger to an even greater one?

Chapter 15
Maria's Hideout

The alley behind the museum wasn't wide, just enough for the sun to throw slivers of light between the shadows of old buildings. Deacon's pulse pounded in his ears, the adrenaline from the fight still coursing through him. He glanced at Sean, who looked equally shaken but steady.

"Come on, let's move!" Maria's urgent voice snapped him back to reality. Without waiting for a response, she darted to a parked moped hidden between two dumpsters, its bright blue paint chipped from use. Deacon hesitated for only a second before deciding to trust her.

"Hop on!" Maria waved him over. Deacon threw a quick look at Hugo, who nodded. Sean climbed into the Jeep beside Hugo, who gunned the engine to life with a roar.

The alley filled with the growl of approaching motorcycles—the Order agents hadn't given up. Deacon swung his leg over the moped behind Maria, barely gripping the handles before she hit the gas. The small bike lurched forward, sending them rocketing out of the alley and into the bustling streets of Montego Bay.

Maria weaved through the traffic with the skill of someone who knew the streets like the back of her hand. Deacon clung to the back of the seat, his knuckles white. He glanced behind them, seeing Sean and Hugo tailing closely in the Jeep, with the Order agents not far behind on their motorcycles. They hadn't lost them yet.

Ahead, the vibrant colors of the city's market district blurred by. Vendors shouted, pedestrians scurried across streets, and the scent of ripe fruits filled the air. Deacon saw one of the Order agents gaining speed behind the Jeep, his motorcycle slipping easily between cars.

"They're getting closer!" he yelled over the wind.

Maria looked back for just a second before swerving sharply, avoiding a vendor's cart loaded with oranges. The cart tipped over, sending a cascade of fruit rolling into the street behind them. Deacon watched as one of the motorcycles swerved to avoid the mess, clipping a parked car and veering off balance.

It wasn't enough to stop them.

"Hold on!" Maria shouted.

Before Deacon could react, Maria turned sharply down a set of stone steps leading to a lower street. The moped bounced down each step, jarring Deacon so hard he thought his teeth would fall out of his head. Behind them, the Jeep couldn't follow, so Hugo turned down a side street instead, disappearing from view for the moment.

The motorcycle following them didn't hesitate. The rider gunned his engine, attempting to take the steps like Maria had. The bike followed, bouncing heavily down the rough stone steps but maintaining control.

Reaching the bottom of the steps, the two bikes gained speed as the terrain leveled out. But the nimble moped was no match for the powerful engine of the street bike and the motorcycle carrying the Order agent quickly caught up to the pair. The rider pulled up close, a black gloved hand reaching out to grab Deacon's arm.

"Get off me!" Deacon shouted, twisting away.

Maria made a sharp right turn, pulling Deacon out of the driver's grasp. The motorcycle followed through the turn just a bit wider than the moped, the driver failing to realize that this particular junction coincided with a large public fountain. The front end of the powerful bike struck the stone base of the fountain, throwing the rider through the air. Birds who, moments before, had been greedily pecking at crumbs dropped along the sidewalk, took flight, and patrons at a nearby café jumped from their tables, shouting in surprise.

Maria barely spared the crash a glance as they zipped through the now-crowded street. But the second Order agent wasn't far behind. He dodged a few pedestrians, maneuvering through the narrow alleyways with practiced precision.

"He's still on us!" Deacon yelled, turning back to see the motorcycle closing in again.

Maria grit her teeth, swerving the moped through a tight corner and nearly clipping a fruit vendor's stall. The motorcycle roared after them, drawing closer with each second. Deacon's heart raced as the Order agent leaned forward, preparing to make his move.

Suddenly, out of nowhere, a large delivery truck pulled out from an alley. Maria seized the moment, veering sharply into a side street just as the truck blocked the road completely. The motorcycle screeched to a halt, the rider forced to slam on his brakes, narrowly avoiding the truck. The Order agent cursed, turning his bike around, but by then Maria had already lost him in the twisting streets.

Deacon let out a breath he hadn't realized he'd been holding.

"That was close."

Maria pulled over into a quieter area, her chest rising and falling rapidly from the excitement of the chase. "Call Hugo," she said, pulling out her phone. "Tell him to meet us at the address I'm about to give you."

Deacon quickly dialed Hugo and relayed the information, his mind still spinning from the events of the past few minutes. Hugo confirmed he was on his way.

The moped weaved through the last few streets before Maria pulled up to a small outbuilding on the campus of the local university. It looked like an old tool shed, the kind that would have gone unnoticed by most passersby. Maria parked the moped and led Deacon inside.

As soon as they entered, Deacon's jaw dropped. The small space was crammed with high-tech computer gear—multiple monitors, a mini-fridge, and the walls were plastered with posters of video game characters, old maps, and coding sheets. It looked like the workspace of someone who knew their way around a circuit board.

"Home sweet home," Maria said with a smirk, dropping her bag onto a nearby chair.

Sean and Hugo arrived moments later, stepping inside with wary glances around the room. Sean immediately perked up, clearly impressed by the setup. "This place is awesome!"

Maria crossed her arms, her expression serious. "Okay, now that we're safe, you guys need to tell me what's going on. Who were those guys? And what's this all about?"

Hugo shot Deacon a look, clearly uncertain how much to reveal. Finally, he sighed. "There's a group of people after something dangerous—something we need to stop them from getting."

Maria raised an eyebrow. "Dangerous how?"

Deacon stepped forward, feeling the weight of the situation. "There's an artifact—an ancient pendant. It's been hidden for centuries, and if they find it, they'll be able to use it to control people. That's what those guys are after."

Maria arched an eyebrow. "What, like a magical pendant with superpowers? Come on, you can't expect me to believe that."

Sean jumped in before Hugo could answer. "It's not magic. We think the pendant is some sort of chemical-based artifact. It affects people's brains, makes them open to suggestion—like a super-hypnotic agent."

Maria blinked, processing this information. "So… a pendant that brainwashes people? That's what those guys are after?"

Hugo nodded grimly. "And now that you've helped us, they'll be after you too."

Maria's eyes flickered with uncertainty, but instead of backing down, her expression hardened. "Well, if they're going to come after me anyway, I might as well help you stop them. And besides, you're not going to find Teach's Cave without me."

Deacon frowned. "Why's that?"

Maria smirked. "Because I know this island better than any tourist map. There's no road to Teach's Cave. You need someone who can navigate the terrain—and I'm your best shot."

Hugo exchanged a glance with Deacon, still looking reluctant, but he knew they didn't have a choice. "Fine," he said. "But this isn't a game. It's dangerous, and we don't know how far the Order will go to get what they want."

Maria grinned, a determined look in her eyes. "I kind of figured that out when I knocked that dude to the ground."

As they prepared to leave, Deacon found himself wondering if he had made the right decision. Maria was smart, no doubt about it, but was it fair to drag her into this? Had he just put one more person at risk? Only time would tell.

Chapter 16
Teach's Cave

The morning sun cast a warm glow over the beach as Deacon, Sean, Maria, and Hugo made their way toward the cliffside where Teach's Cave was hidden. The waves lapped gently at the shore, the air salty and humid. Deacon's heart pounded in his chest, half in anticipation, half in trepidation. They were so close now.

The entrance to the cave was nothing more than a small opening in the rock, obscured by vines and vegetation. Hugo pushed the thick vines aside, revealing the narrow passage.

"This is it," Hugo said, his voice barely above a whisper. "Stay close, and watch your step."

They entered single file, the passage so tight that Deacon had to turn sideways at times to squeeze through. The rocky walls were damp, dripping with moisture from the sea. The tunnel twisted and turned, and it felt like they were descending deeper into the earth. Finally, the narrow tunnel opened into a large cavern, dimly lit by shafts of sunlight filtering through cracks in the rock above.

A small underground lake shimmered at the center of the

cave, its waters still and dark. An old, rotting rowboat lay half-submerged on the shore, and debris from the sea—driftwood, broken glass, and bits of seaweed—littered the ground. The air was cool, carrying the faint scent of saltwater and decay.

"Look at this place," Sean muttered, shining his flashlight around the cavern. "It's like time forgot it."

They spent the next hour combing through the cave, searching for any sign of Caleb Brewster or the pendant. But the cave seemed empty, abandoned. Deacon's excitement began to fade, replaced by frustration. Was this really the place Brewster had hidden the pendant?

"I don't see anything," Maria said, kicking aside a piece of driftwood. "Are we sure this is the right cave?"

Deacon frowned. "It has to be. The coordinates were exact."

Just as they were about to give up, Sean's flashlight flickered over the far wall, catching on something just above head height. A small outcropping of rock, covered in thick vines, protruded from the wall.

"Wait a second," Sean said, stepping closer. "Look at this."

He climbed up the rock face, pushing aside the vines to

reveal a small, hidden passageway just big enough for them to crawl through.

"This looks promising," Hugo said, his tone cautious but intrigued.

One by one, they crawled through the narrow opening, emerging into a smaller chamber on the other side. The air was thicker here, stale and undisturbed. Carved into the stone wall was a small hole, barely noticeable unless you were looking for it.

Hugo knelt down, reaching into the hole. His fingers brushed against something soft and dry. Slowly, he pulled out a bundle wrapped in oilskin.

Deacon's breath caught in his throat. "Is that...?"

Hugo nodded, carefully unwrapping the bundle. Inside was a worn, weathered journal. The pages were yellowed with age, but still intact.

"It's Brewster's diary," Hugo said, handing it to Deacon.

Deacon took the diary, his hands trembling slightly as he opened it. The pages were filled with hastily scrawled handwriting, the ink faded but legible. As they read through the entries, the pieces of the puzzle began to fall into place.

September 1780

Uncle Robert has given me a task of great importance. Although I do not know the significance of this pendant, I will do my best to secure it in the cause of liberty. To keep it safe, I have decided to wear the pendant while aboard ship so that it is not lost while we are at sea.

October 1780

As we continued south, I took notice as we passed Hawksbill Isle. A forlorn scrap of rock where I spent many a night anchored, avoiding the prying eyes of the British as I brought goods in for Uncle Robert. The island's rocky shores made for good cover, though I'd hardly call it a place to linger. It's a barren spit of land with little to offer but shelter from the law. Still, I couldn't help but feel a pang of nostalgia as we passed it by. How many nights had I spent there, hiding under cover of darkness, smuggling in goods that would never be seen by the taxman? It served me well once, but I doubt there's much use for such a place now.

November 1780
I have noticed something strange on this trip. My luck at cards has been incredibly good every time I play while wearing the pendant. It truly is my good luck charm.

January 1781
Having made port in Kingston, I made my way north as instructed to the settlement of Montego. I have decided to delay my mission for just a while, choosing to set up a business and take advantage of the newfound power the pendant has given me. I'm sure my uncle would understand.

April 1781
I have become much interested in the legend of Edward Thache! His is such an inspirational story. My influence in the town continues to grow, as does my fortune.

June 1781
That witch! The woman, Abena, from the town said she recognized Eshu's Pendant. She knows its power and is threatening to expose me to the Governor. If I am exposed, they will take the pendant and I will lose everything. And worse yet, I will have failed my uncle and my cause…more than I already have with my greed. I will do as my hero, Edward, and sail to where he met his end. There I will secure this most wretched pendant that has become a curse upon my life.

They looked up from the diary, their faces pale with the weight of what they had just read.

"So, Brewster never hid the pendant," Deacon said, his voice barely above a whisper. "He used it for himself until it consumed him."

Hugo nodded grimly. "It wasn't until he was threatened with losing everything that he remembered why he was supposed to hide it in the first place."

Maria furrowed her brow. "Wait, what does he mean by 'I will do as my hero, Edward, and sail to where he met his end'? Who's Edward?"

Deacon stared at the diary, trying to make sense of it. "He's talking about Edward Teach—Blackbeard. But what does 'where he met his end' mean? Blackbeard died in a battle, right?"

Hugo nodded, folding his arms. "Blackbeard was killed by the British Navy, but Brewster wouldn't have mentioned it if it wasn't important."

Sean's eyes suddenly widened; his voice excited. "I know where! Blackbeard was killed off the coast of North Carolina, near Ocracoke Island. I saw a video about it when I was looking up pirate stuff online."

Hugo's expression shifted, realization dawning on him. "Ocracoke… That's part of the Outer Banks."

Deacon's pulse quickened. "So that's it. Brewster fled Jamaica and sailed to the Outer Banks, to Blackbeard's final resting place."

Sean shook his head. "And now, that's where the pendant is…somewhere in the Outer Banks…"

Before they could say anything more, a crack sounded from above, muffled by the tons of rock overhead. The ground beneath their feet rumbled, dust fell from the ceiling, and the walls of the cave seemed to shake.

"What the—?" Maria exclaimed.

The rumbling grew louder, the sound of rocks shifting and cracking filling the air. Deacon's heart pounded in his chest. The cave was collapsing.

"Move!" Hugo shouted.

They scrambled back toward the passageway, squeezing through the narrow gap and bursting into the larger cavern below the opening's ledge. Though a thick cloud of dust hung in the air, they carefully made their way to the tunnel leading outside. But, as they reached the opening to the passage, they found it blocked by a massive pile of rubble. The only way out was sealed shut.

"We're trapped," Sean said, his voice rising with panic. "We're trapped!"

Deacon's mind raced, his heart pounding. Dust still hung heavy in the air, and the walls continued to tremble. They were running out of time. If they didn't find another way out soon, they might not make it out at all.

Chapter 17
Escape!

The cavern was eerily quiet after the collapse, the only sound the steady drip of water from the cave ceiling. Dust hung in the air, still thick from the rockslide. Deacon's heart pounded in his chest as he struggled to steady his breath. The entrance was completely blocked, and there was no obvious sign of any other way out.

"Everyone okay?" Hugo's voice broke the silence, calm but filled with urgency.

Deacon, Sean, and Maria all nodded, though their eyes were wide with fear. "We're not hurt," Maria said, "but it does seem like we're trapped."

Hugo scanned the cavern, taking stock of their situation. "Okay. Let's take a moment to assess our situation." He knelt down, pulling out the small bottle of water and the two granola bars they had in their supplies. "We have some food and water. No phones because we didn't want to get them wet. Although they wouldn't do much good without reception down here, anyway."

Sean looked around the cavern which suddenly felt much

smaller than when they first arrived. "Come on, boy-oh, he said. It'll be an adventure, he said." Sean shot Deacon a sly grin. "See what you get for listening to me?"

Deacon gave a nervous chuckle, appreciating Sean's effort to keep the mood light despite the dire situation. But the reality was sinking in: they were trapped underground with seemingly no way out.

Hugo was the first to rush toward the pile of rubble blocking the entrance. He ran his hands over the large stones, tugging at one of the smaller boulders wedged in the mass, testing it. But as he pulled, the rocks shifted slightly, sending a cascade of smaller pebbles tumbling down.

"Careful!" Deacon called out, worried that more of the ceiling might collapse if they weren't careful.

Hugo nodded, stepping back to examine the situation. "We can't just sit here," he muttered, wiping the sweat from his brow. "Let's see if we can make a dent in this. Everyone, help me."

Sean, Maria, and Deacon quickly moved to join Hugo, each picking a section of the rubble pile and working to remove stones. They shifted small rocks at first, working together to try and clear a path. But it was slow going, and every time they pulled one piece free, more seemed to fall into its place. Larger boulders loomed above them, too heavy to move without some serious leverage.

After what felt like hours, they had barely made any progress. Sweat dripped down Deacon's face as he tugged at another stubborn rock, his fingers raw from the effort. He glanced at Hugo, whose expression had grown darker with each passing minute.

"This is going to take days, if it's even possible at all," Hugo finally said, his voice heavy with frustration. "We'd need proper tools—maybe even explosives—to get through this."

Maria sat back, wiping her hands on her jeans. "We're trapped, aren't we?"

For a long moment, no one spoke. The weight of their situation began to settle in, suffocating like the thick dust that still hung in the air. The air inside the cavern felt heavy, cooler than before, and the sound of the dripping water seemed louder in the silence.

"We can't give up," Sean said, though his voice lacked its usual bravado. "There's got to be another way out. There has to be."

Hugo stood, nodding resolutely. "Sean's right. Let's spread out and search the rest of the cavern. We're not done yet."

They moved slowly, each of them scouring different parts of the cave, examining the walls and floor for any signs of hidden tunnels, cracks, or crevices that might lead to another exit. Deacon traced his fingers along the rough stone walls, feeling for any draft of air, any change in the texture of the rock that might hint at a passage. The cold dampness of the cave clung to his skin, chilling him despite the physical exertion.

Maria walked along the shoreline of the underground lake, prodding at the debris and driftwood scattered near the water's edge. "None of this could have come through the entrance we used," she called out. "There's no way. It must have come through a long time ago when the opening to the sea was bigger."

Deacon knelt down beside a pile of old driftwood, noticing how some of the pieces were wedged between rocks. He tried to move one, but it wouldn't budge. The water gently lapped at the wood, and something clicked in his mind.

"Hugo, look at this!" Deacon called, motioning to the debris. "These are way too big to have come through the tunnel we entered. And look," he pointed to the small ripples in the water, "there's movement. There's a current."

Hugo hurried over, his eyes narrowing as he followed Deacon's gaze. Without a word, he pulled a scrap piece of paper from his pocket and tossed it into the water. They watched as it floated on the surface for a few moments before it drifted ever so slightly to one side.

"See that?" Hugo said, his voice gaining an edge of hope. "There's a tide. It's small, but it's there. Which means water is coming in from somewhere—and it's not from above."

"There must be an underground source," Maria said, her voice rising with excitement. "If water's coming in, maybe there's a way out!"

Hugo's mind was already working ahead. "The question is, can we find it, and can we get through it?"

Sean stepped closer to the edge of the lake, staring into the dark, still water. "I guess it's time for another swim."

The thought of swimming through a submerged tunnel made Deacon's stomach churn. But what other choice did they have?

"Are any of you strong swimmers?" Hugo asked.

Sean gave a half-hearted shrug. "I'm okay in the water. Grew up a California beach bum, but I'm no pro." He grinned. "Besides, I just ate half a granola bar, so I should probably wait 30 minutes before I get in the water. Wouldn't want to put myself in any dangerous situations."

Maria looked uncertain. "I can swim well enough, but I'm not great underwater."

Deacon's confidence grew slightly. "I'm a pretty strong swimmer. Bob—one of my foster dads—taught me how to dive, too. We did a lot of SCUBA but he taught me the basics of diving without gear as well. He used to be a SEAL."

Hugo's eyes flickered with surprise. "Good. That'll help. We'll have to free-dive and search for the source of the current."

They took turns diving, each one pushing themselves to stay

underwater longer, searching for any sign of a way out. The lake was vast, and the darkness beneath the surface felt oppressive, making each dive feel like a venture into the unknown. The water was cold, and the deeper they went, the more difficult it became to navigate.

Deacon surfaced after his third dive, shaking the water from his face and catching his breath. "I didn't see anything down there," he said, frustration creeping into his voice. The others were tired too, each one rubbing their arms to keep warm. Sean was sitting on the edge, kicking at the water absently, while Hugo prepared for his next dive.

"I'll go again," Deacon said, determination hardening in his chest. He took a few deep breaths, purging his lungs as Bob had taught him, and plunged beneath the surface once more.

The water closed over his head, and the world above faded into a muffled silence. He swam deeper, his hands running over the smooth rock walls, feeling for anything that might give them a clue. It was hard to see more than a few feet ahead, even with the small flashlight clutched in his grip.

As he neared the bottom of the lake, something caught his eye—an outcropping of rock that jutted from the cavern wall, its surface covered with patches of seagrass. Deacon's pulse quickened. He kicked his legs, moving closer to the outcropping. The seagrass seemed ordinary at first, but then something strange happened—the thin strands of grass began to sway gently, drifting in one direction.

Deacon paused, hanging suspended in the water, watching closely. After a few moments, the grass shifted, swaying in the opposite direction. A current. There was a current here, stronger than anywhere else he had felt in the lake.

He swam closer, bringing the flashlight down near the base of the outcropping. Below the ledge, nestled in the dark, was a small gap—just wide enough for a person to swim through. Deacon felt a surge of hope. This had to be it.

He pressed his hand against the rock and peered into the opening. The water flowed steadily through the gap, and beyond it, he could just make out a tunnel extending further into the depths. The current was stronger here, and he could feel it pulling at him, urging him to follow.

But Deacon knew better than to dive blindly into an unknown tunnel without backup. He kicked hard, pushing himself up toward the surface. His chest burned as his lungs begged for air, but he kept swimming until finally, his head broke through the water.

He gasped, sucking in a deep breath of cool, fresh air. The others rushed over, concern etched on their faces.

"What did you find?" Hugo asked, already knowing by the look in Deacon's eyes that he had found something big.

Deacon wiped the water from his face and pointed toward the far end of the lake. "There's a tunnel. It's under a rock ledge down there," he explained, his breath still coming in short bursts. "There's a current—it pulls the seagrass one way and then the other. It's strong down there, and I'm pretty sure the tunnel leads out."

Hugo's eyes narrowed as he processed the information. "You sure?"

Deacon nodded. "Yeah. The opening's tight, but it's headed in the right direction and looks like it opens up into something bigger. The current's flowing toward it, so I think it's our best shot."

Hugo took a moment to consider the situation. They were running out of options, and with the entrance blocked by rubble, this tunnel might be their only chance of getting out alive.

"I'll check it out," Hugo said, already moving back to the water's edge. "If it's passable, we'll follow it."

"No way," Deacon protested. "I found it; I'll go."

But Hugo shook his head. "It's too dangerous to send anyone else in without knowing what we're dealing with. I'm trained for this." Without waiting for further argument, he dove into the water, disappearing beneath the surface.

They waited in silence, counting the seconds. Each tick seemed to echo louder in the cavern, amplifying the gnawing fear that had settled into Deacon's chest.

30 seconds… 60… 90…

The only sound was the slow drip of water from the cave walls, but each second that passed without Hugo resurfacing felt like a hammer pounding at Deacon's resolve.

At two minutes, Sean's voice trembled, breaking the oppressive quiet. "What if he's stuck?"

Deacon's pulse quickened, his chest tightening as dread pooled in his stomach. His mind raced with the possibilities—

Hugo trapped in a narrow passage, running out of air, or worse. He could picture the tunnel closing in, the dark water pulling Hugo deeper.

The knot of panic tightened in his throat. He couldn't lose Hugo. Not like this.

Deacon took a step toward the water, his decision already made. "I'm going in after him," he said, his voice low but firm, a steel edge of determination cutting through the fear.

Sean grabbed his arm, panic flashing across his face. "What if you get stuck too? We won't know what to do."

Deacon looked at Sean, then at Maria, who stood frozen, her face pale in the dim light. They were scared, and he didn't blame them. So was he. But if Hugo didn't make it, none of them were getting out of here alive.

"I can't just wait here," Deacon said, pulling his arm free. "If he's trapped, I can help him. I know I can."

The silence stretched painfully, every second ticking away like a countdown to disaster.

Deacon's heart pounded in his chest. His mind flashed back to everything Hugo had done to keep them safe, how he'd taken the lead when things got tough. He couldn't just stand here and let him drown.

He took a deep breath, then exhaled deeply, forcing all of the air he could out of his lungs before taking one last deep breath. He knew he would need every second of air his body would give him. He was just preparing to dive in when a faint ripple disturbed the surface of the water. Then, with a gasp, Hugo's head broke through the water.

Before anyone could protest, Deacon took a deep breath, purged all the air from his lungs as Bob had taught him, and dove into the water.

Just as he was about to disappear beneath the waves, Hugo's

head broke the surface, gasping for air. For a second, Deacon couldn't process what he was seeing. Relief hit him so hard he felt his knees almost buckle. He let out a breath he hadn't realized he was holding, a sharp exhale that made his entire body sag.

All three teens rushed to the edge of the water, their voices erupting in a flood of overlapping questions.

"Hugo, are you okay?" Sean blurted, wide-eyed. "What took so long? Did you bring back snacks?" he added, recovering a little bit of his humor.

"Did you find a way out?" Maria added, her voice tight with worry.

"Is it safe?" Deacon asked, his pulse still racing, though the panic was fading. His mind was catching up to the fact that Hugo was back—alive.

Hugo nodded between deep breaths, his face pale but resolute. He motioned for them to give him a moment to catch his breath, but the small smile tugging at the corner of his mouth reassured them that things weren't as dire as they'd feared.

Hugo nodded, breathless but unharmed. "It's doable. About 25 yards to another chamber, then another tunnel, but that one's shorter. We can make it, but it'll be tight."

Deacon relayed the information to the others, and they prepared for the dive. One by one, they practiced the breathing exercises Deacon had been taught, getting ready for the most terrifying swim of their lives.

Deacon led the way, followed closely by Sean, Maria, and Hugo. The first tunnel was pitch black, and Deacon had to swim by feel, his fingers brushing the rocky walls as they moved forward. The water pressed in on all sides, and the distance felt like forever.

Suddenly, Deacon felt a tug on his ankle. He turned as best he could in the tight space to see Sean stuck, his foot caught in a rock crevice. Panic surged in Deacon's chest as he swam back, working furiously to free his friend.

By the time Hugo arrived to help, both Deacon and Sean were running low on oxygen. With Hugo's help, they freed Sean's foot and began swimming for the faint light still agonizingly far away.

The burning in his lungs grew, Deacon's vision began to blur, and his chest screamed for air. Panic rose up in his mind, fighting with the reasonable part of his brain that was telling him to just keep kicking. Fear began to overtake him, and he began to doubt he had the strength or the courage to continue.

A voice, somewhere in the back of his mind, spoke to him and he remembered something his dad had told him years ago: "Bravery is not a lack of fear; it is the recognition that fear exists and deciding to move forward anyway."

With one final surge of strength, Deacon kicked forward, pulling Sean beside him with Hugo helping on the other side. Together, they swam the last few yards and broke the surface of the next chamber, gasping for air.

After taking several moments to catch their breath...and their composure, the four made the final swim through the second, mercifully short tunnel and emerged into a teardrop shaped sapphire pool, the sea held at bay by a rock formation extending partway across the lip of the natural pond formation. The sun was blinding after so many hours spent underground but the fresh air was a relief, and the sight of the beach only a few hundred yards away was one of the most beautiful sights Deacon had ever seen.

As they made their way to the shore, Deacon's eyes drifted back to the cave entrance. Black scorch marks marred the cliffside walls, unmistakable signs of an explosion—the Order had deliberately trapped them inside. Approaching the jeep, Hugo stopped them several yards from the vehicle. The driver's door was standing open, the seat clearly visible. Stuck to the gray leather of the headrest, held in place by a long black handled dagger was a stark white piece of paper.

Cautiously, they walked to the open door, on the lookout for any traps. Drawn on the paper was a crest of some kind. A stag on top of a V-shaped shield, with a gothic "H" inscribed in the center. Hugo's eyes darkened; his lips compressed into a tight line. "Von Heger," was all he said.

This was no game. The Order was playing for keeps.

Deacon exchanged a glance with Sean. There was nothing left for them in Jamaica. It was time to head north, to the Outer Banks—and to the final resting place of a legendary pirate.

Chapter 18
Taking Flight

The sun was setting over Montego Bay as the group arrived at a small, private airstrip, far from the prying eyes of the Order's informants. The tropical heat still clung to the air, but the tension within the group felt heavier than ever. After the cave-in, the chase, and the ominous message left on the Jeep, they all needed a moment to breathe. But there was no time for that. The Order was still after them, and Von Heger was in the shadows, waiting to strike.

Deacon stood beside the sleek, silver jet parked on the tarmac, a stark contrast to the rundown hangar behind it. He'd never seen a private plane up close, let alone considered flying in one. The sight of it felt surreal, like something from a movie, but it only hammered home the reality of how deep the Guardians' reach went.

"You don't like using the jet, do you?" Deacon asked, noticing Hugo's grim expression as he checked his phone.

Hugo sighed, tucking the device back into his pocket. "Not really. It's bad for the environment. We try to avoid unnecessary emissions whenever we can, but in situations like this, we have no choice. The Order has eyes on every major airport and port, so this is the only way to keep you off their radar."

Maria, leaning against the wing, raised an eyebrow. "I didn't think the Guardians had that kind of flex. A private jet? Seriously?"

Hugo smirked slightly, though his eyes remained sharp with focus. "You'd be surprised. The Guardians have been around for centuries. We've accumulated resources—land, wealth, influence. A lot of it's been used to fund covert operations, protect knowledge, and, yes, keep our agents safe when needed. It's how we stay one step ahead of the Order."

Deacon crossed his arms, trying to wrap his head around it. "So... all this time, we've had this secret group fighting to keep civilization from falling apart? And they're, what? Running a hedge fund on the side?"

Hugo chuckled, though the seriousness in his tone never wavered. "It's a bit more complicated than that. The Guardians weren't just about keeping secrets; they were about ensuring that the world didn't fall into chaos. Back in the day, we traded goods, invested in land and industries that were vital to keeping economies stable. It wasn't just about making money—it was about making sure civilization kept progressing."

Deacon raised an eyebrow. "What, like stocks and bonds?"

Hugo shook his head. "Not exactly. The Guardians have been backing major organizations since the Middle Ages. Ever heard of the Knights Templar?"

Sean's eyes lit up. "Wait, you're saying you guys were in with the Templars?"

"More than in with them," Hugo said. "We helped fund them. The Templars were originally a group of warrior monks tasked with protecting pilgrims traveling to the Holy Land, but they essentially invented modern banking. They held and transferred wealth across countries and continents, all while defending civilization. The Guardians provided the backing for their operations."

Deacon blinked, stunned by the revelation. "So the Guardians were basically the Templars' financiers?"

Hugo nodded. "And not just the Templars. There were other groups too—some you've never heard of because they operated in the shadows, like the Order of St. Alaric, a secret group of merchants and tradesmen. They amassed power through discreet means, controlling key trade routes across Europe and the Middle East. Through these groups, the Guardians gained significant wealth and influence over time."

Maria shook her head, half-amused. "So... a secret society funding other secret societies. How very meta."

Hugo's smirk returned. "You could say that. But through these organizations, the Guardians were able to amass considerable holdings—land, gold, art—much of which still funds our operations today."

Deacon nodded slowly, processing the weight of what he'd just learned. "So that's how the Guardians stayed so powerful."

Hugo gave a solemn nod. "It's not just about wealth. It's about the ability to steer civilization when it starts to go off course. The Order seeks to control, but we seek to protect."

Before they could continue, Maria's voice cut through the conversation. "Hey, so... I guess this is where we say goodbye." She crossed her arms, her eyes flicking between Deacon, Sean, and Hugo.

Deacon felt a pang of guilt. They had been through so much together already, and it felt strange to leave Maria behind. "We'll keep you updated," he promised.

Hugo stepped forward and handed Maria a small, sleek phone. "It's encrypted. Use it to stay in touch. If we need anything hacked—or if you find out anything—you can reach us through this."

Maria took the phone, pocketing it with a nod. "Don't worry. I'll be available whenever you need me. I'm not out of this fight yet."

Sean gave her a half-smile. "Don't go knocking over any random thugs while we're gone."

She grinned, punching him lightly on the arm. "Won't need to if there are no 'dudes in distress' hanging around."

Deacon couldn't shake the bittersweet feeling as they said their goodbyes. They had relied on Maria more than once, and it felt strange to leave her out of the next leg of the journey. But they had no choice.

"We'll see you soon," Deacon promised as they boarded the jet.

As they ascended the steps to the plane, Sean leaned in toward Hugo, his expression serious. "We know the pendant's somewhere in the Outer Banks, but it's not like we're doing a scavenger hunt at the local mall…that place is huge. How are we supposed to narrow it down?"

Hugo frowned, running a hand through his hair. "You're right. We've got a lot of ground to cover. Once we're there, we'll need to cross-reference everything—Brewster's journal, Cump's research, and any local information we can find. We have some clues, but we'll have to move fast. The Order's always right behind us, and this time we can't afford any mistakes."

Deacon glanced out the window, his thoughts drifting as they prepared for takeoff. The pieces of the puzzle were slowly coming together, but they still lacked crucial information. They didn't know exactly where to look in the Outer Banks, and if Von Heger was as ruthless as Hugo said, the Order wouldn't give them much time before making their next move.

The jet engines roared to life, and Hugo's voice softened as he looked at Deacon. "The Guardians' wealth isn't just from history or luck. It comes from sacrifices. People like your uncle, who gave everything to protect what's right. We've built this organization for moments exactly like this—to stop people like Von Heger, no matter the cost."

Deacon felt a heaviness settle in his chest. He'd always known the Guardians had a legacy, but now it was becoming clear how much his family had sacrificed. His uncle had given his life for this cause, and now that responsibility seemed to be falling on him.

Hugo checked his watch, breaking Deacon's thoughts. "We'll be landing soon. Once we're in North Carolina, the real work starts. The Order's likely watching, but with any luck, they still think we're in Jamaica. I've got a contact in the Outer Banks who can help us stay off the grid while we figure out our next move."

Deacon nodded, feeling the weight of what lay ahead. It was a race against time, and the Order wasn't far behind.

As the plane cruised through the darkening sky, Deacon's thoughts kept circling back to his uncle's journal, the map, and the mission in front of them. They'd uncovered so much already, but the hardest part still lay ahead. The Order was closing in, and soon enough, the final confrontation would begin.

Chapter 19
The Tinfoil Fisherman

Outer Banks, North Carolina

The sky was streaked with shades of orange and purple as the jet touched down on a small, private airstrip just off the coast of North Carolina. The Outer Banks sprawled out before them, a patchwork of rolling dunes and sandy shores. The soft, salty air was a stark contrast to the humidity of Jamaica, and Deacon couldn't help but feel like they'd crossed into a different world entirely.

As they disembarked the plane, Hugo glanced at his phone, frowning slightly before slipping it back into his jacket pocket. He turned to the group. "I've arranged for a... friend to meet us here. He'll take us to a safe place where we can regroup."

Deacon raised an eyebrow. "A friend?"

Sean nudged him, grinning. "What kind of 'friend' hangs out in a place like this?"

Hugo sighed, rubbing his temples. "Let's just say he's... reliable. But don't expect him to be normal."

A few minutes later, a battered old pickup truck rolled up to the edge of the airstrip, creaking as it slowed to a stop. The door swung open with a loud groan, and out stepped a man in his sixties, wearing a faded fishing hat and a well-worn jacket patched with random bits of fabric. His gray hair stuck out in wild tufts, and a pipe dangled from his lips. Despite the haphazard appearance, his sharp blue eyes surveyed the group with suspicion.

"Y'all the ones lookin' to lay low?" the man asked, his voice gravelly from years of tobacco and salt air.

Hugo stepped forward. "Captain Jack Mercer," he said, nodding curtly. "Thanks for meeting us."

Jack squinted at Hugo before breaking into a wide grin, showing off a set of uneven teeth. "Hugo Deroche! Well, if it ain't the fancy man back on my humble shores again. I didn't think they'd let you out of your little secret bunker these days. Government's probably got all kinds of tabs on you. Aliens, too." He winked at Deacon and Sean, then leaned in conspiratorially. "You know about the aliens, right?"

Sean blinked, barely suppressing a grin. "Aliens?"

"Oh yeah," Jack said, nodding enthusiastically. "They been showin' up more and more around these parts. You see those lights over the dunes at night? Ain't no lighthouse. It's them. And you know the government's in on it, too. They got bases under the ocean. I've seen 'em with my own eyes."

Hugo pinched the bridge of his nose, clearly regretting his choice of contact. "Jack, we don't have time for—"

"And don't even get me started on the secret societies!" Jack interrupted, his voice rising as he waved a hand in the air. "Them shadowy folks? They're everywhere. Pullin' strings, controllin' world leaders. There's this one group, what's it called? The Order? Yeah, them. And don't act like you don't know, Hugo. Bet you're mixed up in all that, too."

Deacon's eyes widened slightly. "Uh, you said the Order?"

"Yep," Jack said, his tone suddenly serious. "Been hearin'

rumors for years. They've got fingers in everything—politics, business, military. You name it, they're there. Only reason I ain't gotten too close is 'cause they know I'm onto 'em." He tapped the side of his head knowingly.

Sean stifled a laugh, nudging Deacon. "This guy's amazing."

Hugo shot them both a warning look. "Don't encourage him."

Jack slapped Hugo on the back, making him stumble slightly. "Ah, lighten up, Deroche. It's good to see you. Now come on, I'll take you to my place. Got a nice spot right on the water—perfect for layin' low."

They piled into the truck, Deacon and Sean exchanging amused glances as Jack rambled on about government surveillance, alien abductions, and how the moon landing was just a diversion so they could build secret bases on the dark side of the moon. Hugo sat in silence, staring straight ahead with a look of long-suffering patience.

After a bumpy ride through the sandy roads of the Outer Banks, they pulled up to a small, weathered house perched on a rocky outcrop overlooking the sea. The house itself looked like it had been pieced together from driftwood and whatever else the tide had brought in, but it had a certain charm to it.

Jack hopped out of the truck, gesturing to the house. "Ain't much, but it's home. Government don't come around here much. And if they do, I got a few tricks up my sleeve."

Deacon stepped out of the truck, taking in the view of the ocean beyond. Despite Jack's wild stories, the place did feel secluded—perfect for what they needed.

Hugo gave Jack a stern look. "We'll only be here a short while. We're trying to locate something in the Outer Banks, and we need to keep a low profile."

Jack grinned, tapping the side of his nose. "Say no more.

I know the drill. You just tell me where you're goin' and I'll make sure no one follows."

As they unloaded their bags, Deacon couldn't help but feel a strange sense of comfort in Jack's eccentric company. Sure, the guy was paranoid, but there was something oddly reassuring about the way he talked about secret conspiracies. Maybe it was because, for the first time, Deacon realized that some of those "crazy" ideas weren't so crazy after all.

Sean leaned over, whispering, "You think he knows about the Guardians?"

Deacon shrugged, smirking. "Who knows? But I bet he's got some stories that come close."

Hugo, however, was not as amused. "Just... try to keep him focused," he muttered. "The last thing we need is him going off on a tangent while we're trying to work."

As they settled into Jack's house, the sun dipped below the horizon, casting the Outer Banks in shadow. Deacon looked out at the dark water, knowing their time was running short. Somewhere out there, the Order was waiting, watching.

But for now, they had a small advantage—and an ally in Jack Mercer, however unconventional he might be.

Jack stood in the doorway, his silhouette framed by the dim light of the porch. "So, what are we lookin' for out there? Buried treasure? Sunken ships?"

Deacon exchanged a glance with Sean, a smile tugging at the corner of his lips. "Something like that."

Chapter 20
The Hunter's Patience

Von Heger's Castle, Bavaria

In the dim, opulent study of the Von Heger ancestral castle, heavy curtains blocked out what little light the overcast sky offered. The room was a relic of centuries past—dark oak paneling, shelves lined with ancient tomes, and a massive, carved stone fireplace where embers smoldered quietly. Above the fireplace, the family crest—a stag on a V-shaped shield—stood in stark contrast to the shadows.

Von Heger sat in a high-backed leather chair, his hands steepled as he stared into the flames, lost in thought. The flickering firelight danced across the tapestries that adorned the walls, casting long shadows, but none so long as the one that had loomed over the Koster family for generations.

The shrill ring of his secure line cut through the quiet. He answered without hesitation.

"Ja?"

"Sir." The voice on the other end belonged to one of his most trusted agents, stationed in North Carolina. "We've confirmed the report. Deroche and the boy survived the cave-in."

Von Heger closed his eyes, leaning back in his chair. A smile tugged at the corner of his lips, though it didn't reach his eyes. "Natürlich they survived. I hoped as much." He rose from his chair, walking to the window that overlooked the mist-covered forests below. "Did they find my message?"

"Yes, sir. The symbol you had us leave on the Jeep—it was seen. But there's more. They've left the island. We don't know where they've gone."

The smile vanished, replaced by a cold, calculating frown. His fingers tightened on the windowsill as he looked out across the sprawling estate. So, Deroche had taken them off the grid. Of course, he had. Hugo always did have a way of slipping out of traps.

"They escaped Jamaica," Von Heger repeated, his voice barely a whisper, more to himself than to his subordinate. "How?"

"Private flight, we believe. But we've been unable to track their destination through our usual channels. They didn't go through the commercial airports."

Von Heger turned back toward the fire, the wheels in his mind already spinning. "Get our contacts to hack the private flight plans. I want their destination before the day is out."

"Sir, it may take some time. The systems are...complex. But we're on it."

The veins in Von Heger's temple pulsed, though his voice remained even. "Then I suggest you begin immediately. Zeit ist Macht—time is power. I want their location."

He disconnected the call, tossing the phone onto his desk. His fingers drummed against the dark wood, mind swirling with the implications. Deroche had managed to evade his men in Jamaica and now the boy—Koster's nephew—was slipping further from his grasp. He had underestimated the tenacity of these children, a mistake he would not repeat.

The fact that they had fled the island so swiftly troubled him. There were too many moving parts, too many unknowns. Wherever they were headed, it would only take them closer to the talisman. Von Heger could feel it in his bones.

His eyes drifted up to the stag crest again. The feud between their families had gone on for centuries, but it had become far more personal since the last time a Koster had brought ruin to his family. His father, outed as an East German spy decades ago by Deacon's great uncle, had nearly destroyed everything they'd built. Bavaria—West Germany—had no place for an East German traitor. Every fortune they had, every social tie they'd cultivated, had crumbled in the wake of the scandal. His father's death hadn't been enough to erase the stain on their name. The Von Heger family's reputation within the Order, driven by the humiliation of the very public defeat by their Koster rivals, had never fully recovered. They were barred from the highest echelons of power, relegated to the shadows. And all because of the Koster family's interference. But that would change. He would make sure of it. He would restore their honor, no matter the cost.

That was why the talisman wasn't just another object to him—it was the key to regaining the power his family had lost. The Kosters had held the upper hand for too long. And Von Heger was tired of playing defense.

He strode over to the fireplace and stood in the heat of the embers, feeling the warmth on his skin. If the agents in North Carolina couldn't find the boy quickly, then it was time to get personally involved.

"Enough games," he murmured. "The hounds have failed to corner the hare. It's time the huntsman enters the fray."

Von Heger's gaze hardened as he made the decision. He

would oversee the hunt for the talisman himself. The time for delegating was over. He would crush Deroche and the boy— just as his father should have crushed the Kosters decades ago.

He reached for his phone again, this time calling his personal assistant. "Prepare the jet," he said, his voice like ice. "I'm leaving for America. It's time I finish this."

As the fire crackled in the hearth behind him, the ancient walls of the Von Heger castle seemed to close in, the weight of centuries of rivalry and bloodshed pressing down on his shoulders. But soon, he would stand victorious. The pendant would be his.

And with it, the so would the world.

Chapter 21
A Pirate's Life for Me

Sean sat cross-legged on Captain Jack's weather-beaten porch, staring out at the distant horizon where the deep blue of the ocean met the sky. Deacon and Hugo were inside, hunched over the dining table, discussing the clues they had gathered. Sean had been trying to follow their conversation, but his mind kept drifting back to the image of the pendant. It was there—he could feel it, somewhere close. They were on the edge of something huge.

Deacon's voice cut through the muggy air, snapping Sean out of his thoughts. "Sean? You with us, buddy?"

He blinked, shaking off the haze of his daydream. "Yeah, sorry. What were you saying?"

Hugo frowned, his fingers tracing the edge of a map spread out on the table. "We're trying to narrow down where the pendant could be. We've been through just about every article we could find online about this area during the late 18th Century. Nothing really stands out."

Hugo continued, "We've been looking at everything Cump wrote in his journal and combed through every piece of evidence

Brewster left behind. But we're still missing something."

Sean leaned back against the porch railing, tapping his chin. His mind was still stuck on that journal entry from Brewster. There had been something there—a reference that felt important but hadn't seemed relevant at the time.

"Wait," Sean said, sitting up straight. "Brewster mentioned something, didn't he? Something about an island they passed while sailing south from New York."

Deacon furrowed his brow. "Yeah, Hawksbill Isle. He said it was a good place to hide because of the jagged rocks and secluded coves, but we didn't think much of it. It's not like he made it sound important."

Hugo's frown deepened. "Hawksbill Isle? I remember that from Brewster's entries, but why are you bringing it up now?"

Sean shrugged, but his mind was racing. "Brewster mentioned stopping there when he was smuggling goods for his uncle. That's gotta mean something, right? Maybe it wasn't just a stop on the route—it could have been a place where he stashed things he didn't want the British to find."

Deacon's eyes widened as the pieces began to fall into place. "So, you think the pendant might be there?"

Sean leaned forward, excitement growing. "It makes sense, doesn't it? Brewster was obsessed with Blackbeard—he would have known about the local legends and hiding spots. And remember Cump's journal? He mentioned something about Dead Man's Point being used by smugglers, too. Both Brewster and Townsend were involved in smuggling, and they had to avoid the British at all costs."

Hugo was starting to look intrigued. "Dead Man's Point, Hawksbill Isle… you think they're connected somehow? Both of them being used as hideouts for smugglers, avoiding British tariffs and customs agents?"

Sean nodded eagerly. "Why not? Brewster could've believed that Hawksbill was the perfect place to hide the pendant—especially if Blackbeard had already hidden treasure there. It's isolated, dangerous, and full of history. Maybe he even thought Teach's legend would keep people away from it."

Deacon looked skeptical. "I mean, it's a cool theory, but we're talking about legends here. Ghost stories."

Just then, Captain Jack sauntered out onto the porch, his crooked grin appearing beneath his scraggly gray beard. "I didn't mean to overhear you or anything," he said, eyes twinkling with mischief. "but I couldn't help it seeing as I was listening so hard."

Sean and Deacon traded amused glances.

Jack continued, "Aye, there's a legend 'round these parts that ol' Blackbeard didn't just die at Ocracoke. Some say he stashed a portion of his treasure along the coast before his run-in with the British. Hidden even from his crew, they say. Lot of folks think that spot was on Hawksbill."

Sean's eyes widened. "See? That's exactly what I'm talking about! Hawksbill Isle is perfect for hiding something. Dangerous surf, jagged cliffs. Brewster could've hidden the pendant there, and no one would've thought to look."

Hugo scratched his chin. "I'll admit, it makes sense. But even if it's true, how difficult will it be to get there? Brewster made it sound pretty treacherous."

Captain Jack crossed his arms, his grin fading slightly. "Aye, treacherous indeed. Some folks've tried searchin' that island over the years, but not many come back without a few scrapes and broken bones. Surf that'll toss you around like a golden retriever's chew toy, jagged rocks that can rip the bottom out of your boat 'fore you even know you're on top of them. No, I don't think that's a place I'd like to help you get to."

Hugo raised one eyebrow in question. "Come on, Jack. Are the conditions so bad you won't consider taking us?"

The Captain gave Hugo a look of mild scorn. "There ain't a part of these waters I can't go, sonny."

"Ah," Deroche replied with a smirk. "It's Blackbeard's ghost then. You afraid Teach's ghost will board your boat and make you walk the plank?"

Jack chuckled, a low, raspy sound, and shook his head. "Do you know how ridiculous you sound right now? Everyone knows there are no such things as ghosts." His chuckling subsided, he continued, "No, I won't go out there because of the government."

Sean blinked, glancing at Deacon, who raised an eyebrow. "The government?" Sean asked. "What do they have to do with it?"

Jack looked deadly serious. "The ghost stories are just a cover. Everyone knows Hawksbill Isle's haunted—that keeps the gullible, superstitious folks away. But the real reason nobody goes there is 'cause it's where the government's got their top-secret stealth submarine testing goin' on. Black ops, alien technology, that sort of thing. They don't want nobody pokin' around."

Deacon let out a snort, trying to hide his laughter. "Submarine testing? Really?"

"I'm serious!" Jack said, gesturing wildly with his hands. "They use that island for all kinds of top-secret operations. I've seen some things out there I ain't ever been able to explain. That's why I don't make runs there anymore. Not unless I wanna end up on some government watchlist."

Hugo smirked. "So, that's why you don't want to take us. You're afraid of running into a submarine?"

Jack scowled. "It ain't funny, lad. You don't know what I've seen. But ghost stories and submarines aside, the real problem is those jagged rocks. I can get you to Hawksbill, but I can't guarantee you'll make it back in one piece."

Deacon leaned back in his chair, folding his arms. "If you think it's too dangerous, we'll figure something else out."

Jack hesitated for a moment, glancing between the three of them. He scratched his head, then sighed heavily. "Look, I'll take you. But you best be ready for anything. Once we're on that island, it's you against nature. And if Teach's ghost really is hangin' around, don't come cryin' to me."

Sean grinned. "Don't worry, Jack. We're more worried about what's in front of us than some old pirate ghost."

Deacon added with a nod, "And if it really is the pendant Brewster hid there, we'll need to get in and out fast. There are some people not too not far behind us that probably wouldn't lose a lot of sleep if we ended up joining Teach's ghost out there."

As Jack turned to make preparations for the trip, Sean looked to Deacon and Hugo. "This is it, guys. Hawksbill Isle. The pendant's gotta be there."

Hugo gave a curt nod. "Then we move fast. We don't know how much time we have before the Order catches up. They won't be pleased we gave them the slip in Jamaica, and they will not hesitate to kill any one of us to keep that pendant from falling into Guardian hands."

Sean swallowed hard, a surge of both excitement and dread coursing through him. This was it—potentially their last step in the hunt for Eshu's Pendant. But something told him Hawksbill Isle wouldn't give up its secrets without a fight.

Chapter 22
The Approach

The ocean churned an angry gray flecked with white beneath them as Captain Jack's boat cut through the rolling waves. The sky was overcast, heavy with the threat of a storm. Sean gripped the side of the boat, knuckles white as he tried to keep his balance with each dip and rise of the vessel. Deacon and Hugo sat nearby, eyes fixed on the dark shape of Hawksbill Isle looming ahead.

"This doesn't look good," Sean muttered under his breath as a particularly large wave smacked the side of the boat, sending salty spray across his face.

Captain Jack, standing at the helm with one hand on the wheel and the other gripping his pipe, gave a raspy chuckle. "Good? It's about as good as it gets, lad. We're lucky it's not worse. These waters can chew up a boat and spit it out like a bad piece of meat."

Sean swallowed hard, his stomach lurching as the boat tipped sideways again. "Great. Remind me to go Vegan when we get home."

Hugo glanced back at him, a calm exterior masking the

tension in his eyes. "Just hold on. We're almost there."

Sean wiped his brow, then leaned over to Deacon. "This was your idea, right? Smugglers' hideouts, lost treasures, world-controlling pendant hunting?"

Deacon cracked a grin, though the worry etched into his features was hard to miss. "You're the one who connected the dots. Hawksbill's your idea."

"Yeah, well, I already sent a note to Mr. Oliver saying if anything happens to us, we should be buried beside each other and my tombstone will say 'It was his fault' with an arrow pointing at yours," Sean said, forcing a laugh that was drowned out by the roar of another wave crashing into the side of the boat.

The island grew closer with every minute, its rocky cliffs and jagged coastline becoming clearer. Captain Jack maneuvered the boat expertly, but even he looked tense now as the waves grew more unpredictable, throwing the boat from side to side.

"Careful!" Deacon called out as the boat tipped sharply to one side, nearly sending him sprawling across the deck.

"I'm always careful," Jack replied, eyes narrowing as he steered the boat toward what looked like a narrow gap between two large rock formations. "Hold on tight. This is the tricky part."

Sean glanced at the approaching rocks and felt his heart leap into his throat. The gap looked impossibly small for their boat, and the jagged edges of the formations seemed to be waiting for one wrong move to rip them apart.

"You're kidding, right?" Sean yelled over the roar of the ocean.

Jack shot him a grin over his shoulder, his gold tooth glinting in the fading light. "Relax, kid. I've done this a hundred times."

"Pretty sure we're not talking about times when you were

smuggling treasure hunters to a haunted island," Sean muttered.

Hugo gripped the side of the boat, his eyes locked on the narrow passage ahead. "We're kind of committed at this point. Just trust him."

The boat surged forward, heading straight for the gap. Sean braced himself, his breath held as they approached what felt like certain doom. The jagged rocks seemed to rise up on either side of them, and for a moment, Sean was sure they were going to crash.

Then, with a sudden lurch, the boat slid through the gap, barely missing the sharp rocks by inches. Captain Jack let out a triumphant whoop, steering them into calmer waters on the other side.

"See? Told ya I had it under control," Jack said, puffing out his chest as he steered them toward a small cove nestled between the cliffs of Hawksbill Isle.

Sean exhaled, his muscles unclenching as the boat finally slowed. "You're insane, you know that, right?"

Jack shrugged, a mischievous glint in his eye. "Maybe. But we're here, aren't we?"

Hugo stood, glancing at the cliffs that rose ominously above them. "That was the easy part. Now comes the hard part."

Sean and Deacon followed his gaze, their eyes tracing the rugged terrain of the island. The cliffs were steep, and the jagged rocks below gave no room for error. The waves still battered the shore, sending white foam spraying into the air.

Deacon wiped his face with his sleeve, his jaw tight. "We're really doing this, huh?"

Sean nodded, though his heart pounded in his chest. "Yeah. We're really doing this."

Jack brought the boat to a stop near a rocky outcrop, lowering the anchor with a practiced hand. "I can't take you any closer.

This is where we part ways—for now. You lot be careful up there. Hawksbill doesn't like visitors."

Hugo gave him a nod. "We'll be back soon."

Jack narrowed his eyes. "You better be. These waters get meaner the longer you stay. I'll be waitin'—but I can't promise how long the weather will hold."

Sean glanced up at the sky, noticing for the first time the thickening clouds. "Oh good. I was hoping we could do this in the rain," the sarcasm evident in his monotone delivery.

Deacon climbed to the edge of the boat, tossing a rope to the rocky shore. "Come on. Let's not waste time."

One by one, they scrambled out of the boat and onto the slippery rocks, the wind howling around them as they made their way toward the base of the cliffs. Sean's heart pounded in his ears, but a strange sense of excitement fueled him. This was it. Hawksbill Isle. They were closer than ever to finding the pendant.

But as they started the climb toward the cliffs, a nagging voice in the back of his mind reminded him that they weren't alone. The Order was out there. Somewhere. And they were getting closer.

Chapter 23
The Ascent

Deacon's fingers gripped the rough, wet stone as he hoisted himself onto the narrow path that clung to the edge of the cliff. The wind whipped around them, carrying the smell of salt and the distant rumble of the restless sea. His muscles were already aching from the effort, but there was no time to stop. The cliff loomed above them like a jagged staircase leading to nowhere, and the only way forward was up.

"Keep moving," Hugo called over the wind, his voice steady and calm. He was leading the way, his eyes scanning the cliffside for the best handholds and footholds. Behind him, Sean was quiet for once, focused entirely on not slipping as they made their way along the precarious ledge.

Deacon swallowed, his throat dry despite the damp air. Every step felt more treacherous than the last. The path was barely wide enough for a single foot in some places, and beneath them, the jagged rocks waited like the teeth of some great beast, ready to tear apart anything—or anyone—that fell.

"Why are we doing this again?" Deacon muttered under his breath as he pressed his back to the cliff, inching forward.

Hugo didn't answer right away, but after a moment, he said, "Because we have no other choice. If the pendant is here, it's not going to be easy to find. We just have to trust our instincts. There's always a way forward—you just have to find it."

Deacon wasn't sure if Hugo was talking about the cliff or something bigger, but either way, it didn't make the climb any easier. His boots slipped slightly on the wet rock, and he cursed under his breath, tightening his grip on a jagged outcrop above him.

They continued in silence, the wind howling around them like some unseen predator waiting for one of them to make a mistake. Deacon's mind raced with thoughts of the pendant, the Order, and what would happen if they didn't find it. If the Order got there first...

He pushed the thought aside. There was no room for doubt, not now. Not with the Order breathing down their necks.

"Deacon, focus," Hugo said sharply, glancing back at him. "One step at a time."

Deacon nodded, taking a deep breath. His heart pounded in his chest as he forced himself to keep climbing. They were close, he could feel it. Hawksbill Isle held the answers, he just knew it.

As they rounded a corner, the path narrowed even further, and Deacon's stomach clenched at the sight. The ledge was barely a foot wide now, and the wind was stronger, battering them with gusts that threatened to knock them off balance. Beneath them, the sea roared, its waves crashing against the rocks far below.

"Careful," Hugo said, his voice low and steady. "This part's tricky."

Deacon followed Hugo's lead, his movements slow and deliberate. He could hear Sean muttering something behind him, but the words were lost in the wind. Deacon wasn't in the mood for jokes anymore. All he could think about was the drop below them.

As they crept along the narrow ledge, something caught Deacon's eye. Up ahead, there was a small alcove, tucked into the side of the cliff. It was barely noticeable, hidden in the shadow of the rock face. But there was something about it, something that felt... deliberate.

Deacon edged forward, every muscle in his body tight with concentration as he followed Hugo's lead. The wind was relentless, tearing at his clothes and whipping at his face, but his focus was entirely on the narrow ledge in front of him. His breath came in steady, shallow bursts as he pressed himself closer to the cliffside. They were almost at the alcove, just a little further.

Then, suddenly, the sound of scrambling echoed behind him—stones slipping, feet sliding. Deacon's heart seized in his chest.

"Whoa! Deacon!" Sean's voice, high with panic, ripped through the wind.

Deacon twisted his body just in time to see Sean lose his footing. His boots skidded down the wet rock, his arms flailing as he tried to grab hold of anything solid. For a terrifying moment, Sean teetered at the edge, his body tilting dangerously toward the abyss below.

Deacon's heart stopped. "Sean!"

Sean's hand shot out, finding what remained of the ledge by sheer luck. His fingers curled around a small outcrop of rock, knuckles turning white as he clung to it, legs dangling over the edge.

"Deacon, I—" Sean gasped, his voice ragged with fear, "Help, please!"

Hugo was too far ahead, already at the narrowest part of the ledge where turning back would be impossible. Deacon's mind raced. There would be no other help. It was up to him.

"Hold on, Sean!" Deacon yelled, though his heart was hammering in his chest, panic threatening to overtake him. He scanned the cliffside, searching for anything—anything—he could use to save his best friend.

They had rope. Supplies. Deacon's fingers fumbled at the small pack slung across his back, his breath coming in quick, uneven bursts. Think, Deacon. Think!

In the chaos of his mind, a memory surfaced. His dad, teaching him how to control his breathing in high-stress situations. Combat breathing, they called it. It calms your heart, your mind, keeps the panic at bay.

Deacon closed his eyes, forcing his breath to slow. He counted: in for four, hold for four, out for four. Slowly, his hands steadied. His mind cleared. Focus.

He pulled out the rope from his pack, deftly tying it off to a carabiner. His fingers worked quickly, almost mechanically, as his dad's voice echoed in his mind, guiding him. He wrapped the rope around the heavy-duty flashlight they'd brought—the one with the weight of a solid piece of metal. The flashlight would do. It had to do.

"Deacon!" Sean's voice was strained, his grip slipping.

"I'm coming, Sean. Just hang on!" Deacon shouted back, tying a rescue loop at the other end of the rope. He wedged the flashlight between two solid rocks on the cliffside, testing it with a sharp tug. The flashlight held.

Please hold. Please hold.

Deacon edged closer to Sean, the narrow ledge forcing him to move carefully, all while keeping one hand on the rope. His stomach churned with the fear that Sean wouldn't be able to hold on much longer.

"Sean, grab this!" Deacon called, tossing the rescue loop toward his friend. It dangled just within reach of Sean's outstretched hand.

Sean's fingers brushed the rope but didn't catch. His breath was coming in panicked gasps. "I— I can't reach!"

Deacon felt the cold edge of dread press against him, but he forced it down. "You can reach, Sean. You have to. Just one more try!"

Sean's teeth were gritted in effort, his face pale, but he stretched out his arm again. This time, his fingers curled around the rope.

"I got it!" Sean gasped, wrapping the rope around his wrist as tightly as he could manage.

Deacon planted his feet, his boots digging into the rock as he braced himself. His legs shook from the strain, but he pulled with everything he had. Inch by inch, Sean began to rise, his body slowly pulling away from the deadly drop below.

"Come on, Sean," Deacon muttered through gritted teeth, his muscles screaming as he hauled Sean up the cliffside. The wind howled around them, but Deacon's world had narrowed to just the rope in his hands and the weight of his best friend at the other end.

With one final heave, Sean scrambled onto the narrow ledge, collapsing next to Deacon, both of them panting hard.

Deacon's body felt like jelly, but he managed to force a grin. "You okay?"

Sean lay on his back, staring up at the sky. "Do you think... this theme park...gives refunds?"

Deacon let out a shaky laugh, relief flooding through him as he helped Sean sit up. But the fear still lingered at the edge of his mind, a cold reminder of how close they'd come to disaster.

He glanced up at the narrow ledge ahead of them. "We need to move. Come on."

With Sean safely beside him, they pressed forward toward the alcove. The storm was still brewing above, and danger lurked below, but they had made it through one more challenge together.

The wind was still howling outside, but inside the alcove, it was quiet—almost eerily so. Deacon glanced around, his breath catching in his throat. The walls were smooth, unnaturally smooth for a place like this. And then he saw it—a carving.

Etched into the wall of the alcove, barely visible in the dim light, was a series of lines—jagged and worn from age, yet unmistakably deliberate. Deacon squinted, brushing his fingers across the surface. He stepped back, heart pounding. It wasn't just random scratches—it was writing, though the lines were worn from age. The script formed a riddle.

A riddle meant they were close—close to uncovering whatever had been hidden here, likely by Brewster himself. But a riddle also meant another delay and with a storm brewing outside, the island fighting to hold her secrets and the Order closing in, time was not on their side.

Chapter 24
The Riddle in the Rock

Deacon stood at the entrance of the alcove, his breath still heavy from the climb. The wind howled outside, but the small nook offered respite inside. His eyes locked on the strange, carved lines etched into the wall. The riddle had the same worn look as the rocks around it, like it had been waiting for centuries to be discovered.

> *"Where shadows stretch at the height of day,*
> *In the hidden halls where corsairs lay,*
> *Seek the echoes of those left behind,*
> *In the rock's deep heart, secrets confined.*
> *The cursed key brought at such great cost,*
> *Lies within the Shadow of the Lost."*

Sean stood just behind him, reading over Deacon's shoulder. "A riddle," he said, voice tinged with excitement, but the underlying tension in his words was unmistakable. "This is it. We're close."

Hugo nodded, eyes sharp as he analyzed the riddle. "It's vague enough to keep away someone who didn't know what Brewster was hiding, but specific enough to point in the right direction if you know what you're after."

Deacon traced the words with his fingers, his mind racing. "Shadows stretch at the height of day," he muttered. "That's noon, right?"

"Yeah, which is about right now. But there's no sun," Sean pointed out, glancing up at the thick clouds overhead. The sky was heavy with the promise of a storm, making the day feel as dark as dusk. "No shadows today, not unless we wait until this storm blows over."

Deacon clenched his jaw. They didn't have time to wait. The Order would be catching up to them soon, if they weren't already on the island. His mind raced as he considered the rest of the riddle.

"Seek the echoes of those left behind... shadows of the lost..." Sean rubbed the back of his neck, thinking aloud. "It sounds like we're looking for a place where people used to be... maybe the smugglers. But where would they hide?"

"Someplace protected," Hugo answered, pacing back and forth inside the small alcove. "The cliffs here are treacherous, but they'd also offer shelter from prying eyes. And the rock's deep heart... that has to mean something underground, something hidden within the cliffs themselves."

Deacon felt a surge of frustration. They had the riddle, but no sun to help them find the shadows. They were running out of time. The storm was closing in fast, and the Order couldn't be far behind.

"Okay, let's think this through," Sean said, stepping up beside Deacon. His tone was unusually focused, his usual humor absent. "Even without the sun, the riddle has to mean there's only one place on this island where shadows would stretch at noon. It has to be some sort of rock formation, right? Something that casts a shadow every day."

Hugo nodded. "That would make sense. A natural formation that would create shade, even when the sun's not out."

Deacon scanned the cliffs, his heart pounding in his chest. The rocks were jagged, chaotic, with little to distinguish one outcropping from another. His eyes roved over the ledge they'd just crossed and the towering cliffs beyond, the wind whipping at his hair.

Then something caught his eye. Off to the side, higher up along the cliff face, a rocky overhang jutted out, its shape creating a natural ledge beneath it. Deacon narrowed his eyes. It wasn't casting a shadow now, not with the storm looming, but at noon, with the sun directly overhead...

"That's it," Deacon said, his voice low but firm. He pointed toward the outcropping. "Up there. That's the only place on this island that would cast a shadow at noon."

Sean followed his gaze, squinting at the overhang. "That's a stretch, Deacon. How do you know?"

"I don't," Deacon admitted, "but it's the only thing that makes sense. The rock's deep heart... whatever's hidden has to be inside the cliffs. And if we're looking for a shadow at noon, that outcropping is the only spot that would create one."

Hugo considered Deacon's words for a moment, then gave a sharp nod. "It's worth a shot. Let's move."

The wind had picked up by the time they reached the base of the overhang. Rain had begun to fall, a light drizzle that quickly turned the rocks slick beneath their feet. Deacon's heart pounded as they climbed, each step feeling more precarious than the last.

Sean scrambled up beside him, his breathing heavy as they reached the narrow path that led to the outcropping. "You think this is it?" he asked, his voice barely audible over the wind.

"It has to be," Deacon said, though doubt gnawed at the

edges of his thoughts. This whole hunt had been a series of puzzles, each one more dangerous than the last. But this felt different. This felt final.

They pressed forward, the path growing narrower as they approached the overhang. The rain was coming down harder now, making it difficult to keep their footing. Deacon slipped once, his hand catching on a jagged rock that tore at his skin.

"Careful," Hugo warned from behind them, his voice tense. "This storm's getting worse. We need to hurry."

Deacon grit his teeth, pushing through the pain. They were close. He could feel it. Hawksbill Isle held the answers, he just knew it.

Snatches of a distant thumping sound broke through the noise of the wind and crashing surf. Deacon stopped for a moment, his breath catching in his throat. He strained his ears, but the sound vanished almost as soon as it came. Was it real? Or just the sound of his own heart beating loudly, thudding with the rising tension?

Deacon shook his head, dismissing the thought. It had to be the storm, the wind playing tricks on him.

They were close now. The pendant had to be here.

Deacon stepped into the narrow passage leading down into the cliff. Around 100 yards in, he found their path blocked. A rockfall had collapsed part of the tunnel, leaving a pile of debris that cut off their way forward.

"Great," Sean muttered, glancing back toward the opening. "More rocks. Yippee."

Hugo crouched beside the fallen rocks, running a hand over them. "It's not too bad. We can clear it, but we need to work fast."

Deacon set his jaw, already tugging at the loose stones. The rocks were heavy, the sharp edges biting into his already-raw palms as he heaved them aside, one by one. Sean worked beside him, muttering under his breath as they tossed the debris to the side.

They were a little more than halfway through when another sound filtered down the passage. A distant, muffled noise, growing louder with each passing second.

Deacon froze, his heart skipping a beat. This time, it wasn't just his imagination. He glanced back at Hugo, who had gone still, his expression darkening.

"Voices," Hugo said quietly. "They're close."

Sean swore under his breath, his hands working faster now as he tossed aside the last of the smaller stones. "What are the odds that's just Captain Jack, come to check on us, talking to himself again? Or maybe we got lucky and it's Blackbeard's ghost?"

The voices were getting louder, more distinct. The Order. They were closing in.

Deacon's pulse raced as they cleared the last of the smaller rocks, revealing a narrow opening just big enough for them to squeeze through. "Go," Hugo ordered, waving them forward.

Deacon slid through first, followed by Sean, the tunnel narrowing as they pressed deeper into the cliff. The sound of voices echoed behind them, growing louder with each passing second. They had to move faster.

But as they crawled through the narrow passage, Sean's foot caught on a loose stone, sending a cascade of rocks crashing down behind them.

The sound echoed loudly through the tunnel, unmistakable in its source.

"They'll know where we are now," Hugo hissed, glancing back. "Move. Quickly."

Deacon's heart pounded in his chest as they scrambled

through the tight space, the narrow walls pressing in on either side. They were close to the pendant, but the Order was right behind them—and now, they knew exactly where to look.

Chapter 25
In the Shadow of the Lost

The air inside the tunnel was damp and stale, thick with the scent of earth and ancient stone. Deacon's breathing echoed loudly in the narrow passage, each inhale and exhale amplifying the already suffocating tension. Behind him, Sean and Hugo moved in near silence, their footsteps scraping on the uneven ground.

After what felt like an eternity of squeezing through the tight spaces, the narrow path finally opened into a larger chamber. Deacon stopped short, his eyes widening as the dim light from Hugo's flashlight illuminated the space ahead.

The cavern was vast, its stone walls stretching high above them, disappearing into the shadows. At the far end, a small recess was carved into the rock face, almost invisible in the gloom. It was small, almost unassuming, but Deacon could feel the weight of history in the air around it, as though the very stone itself gained strength from the passage of time, guarding the secrets within.

"This has to be it," Sean whispered, stepping up beside Deacon, his voice hushed in the stillness. "This is where

Brewster hid the pendant."

They were close now. The pendant had to be here.

But between them and the alcove was a narrow ledge, barely wide enough for a foot to rest comfortably. Below the ledge, a drop descended into complete darkness. The flashlight's beam didn't even reach the bottom. Deacon's stomach twisted at the thought of what lay beneath—jagged rocks, a fall too deep to survive, or worse.

"Careful," Hugo murmured, stepping forward to survey the situation. "One wrong step, and that ledge will take you down with it."

Deacon's pulse quickened as his eyes darted from the ledge to the alcove. The pendant was within reach, but it would take a steady hand—and a lot of nerve—to cross that deadly stretch of rock.

Hugo took the first step, moving cautiously, testing each stone before shifting his weight. The sound of small pebbles skittering off the edge of the ledge sent a shiver up Deacon's spine. He followed closely behind, his heart pounding in his chest. Every step felt like walking on the edge of a knife, the stones beneath their feet shifting slightly with each movement.

About halfway across, Sean's foot slipped, sending a cascade of loose stones clattering into the abyss. Deacon's heart lurched, his hand instinctively reaching out to steady Sean before he lost his balance completely.

"You good?" Deacon asked, his voice barely a whisper.

Sean swallowed hard, his face pale in the dim light. "Yeah... yeah, I'm good."

They pressed forward, their movements slow and deliberate. The air felt heavier the closer they got to the alcove, as though the weight of centuries was pressing down on them, urging them to turn back, to leave the pendant buried in the shadows where it had been hidden for so long.

Finally, they reached the stony recess. It was smaller than Deacon had expected, barely large enough for him to fit his arm inside. His hand trembled slightly as he reached out, brushing his fingers over the rough stone.

"There," Hugo said, pointing to a small gap in the rock. "That's where it is."

Deacon crouched down, carefully maneuvering his arm into the gap. His fingers searched the cold stone, feeling the jagged edges of the rocks. For a moment, he thought it was empty—that they had come all this way for nothing. But then, his fingers brushed against something smooth and cool.

He wrapped his hand around it, pulling it free from the stone's embrace. The pendant was small, no larger than a coin, but it shimmered faintly in the dim light, its surface etched with symbols that Deacon couldn't quite make out. The leather cord falling to pieces where two and half centuries of damp had caused it to rot away.

"We've got it," Deacon breathed, holding the pendant up for Sean and Hugo to sec.

But the instant the pendant left the alcove, the ground beneath them trembled. A low rumble echoed through the chamber, the stones beneath their feet vibrating as if the island itself had come alive.

"What was that?" Sean asked, his voice tight with fear.

Before Deacon could answer, a loud crash came from behind them—the sound of footsteps, heavy and determined, echoing through the tunnel.

Hugo's face darkened, his eyes narrowing. "The Order."

Without warning, three Order operatives burst into the chamber, their flashlights cutting through the darkness like knives. Deacon's heart raced, his grip tightening on the pendant.

There was no time to think, no time to plan. They had to move.

"Go!" Hugo barked, turning to face the approaching agents as Deacon and Sean scrambled back toward the narrow ledge.

The sound of gunfire ricocheted through the chamber, bullets striking the stone walls as Deacon and Sean darted across the ledge. Deacon's heart pounded in his ears, his breath coming in sharp gasps as he pushed himself forward, his eyes fixed on the path ahead.

But the rocks were crumbling beneath them, breaking away as they ran. The ledge was collapsing, piece by piece, and there was no time to stop.

Deacon's foot slipped, the stone beneath him giving way. For a heart-stopping moment, he teetered on the edge of the abyss, his arms flailing as he tried to regain his balance.

"Deacon!" Sean's voice was distant, barely audible over the roar of the collapsing stones.

Deacon's hand shot out, grasping at a jagged outcrop of stone just as the ledge beneath him crumbled into darkness. His fingers screamed in protest, muscles cramping as he hung there, but he held on, his heart pounding in his ears.

Bullets chipped the rock wall around them, sending shards of stone scattering over the trio. The ledge continued to disintegrate, inching closer to where Sean and Hugo stood frozen, danger drawing nearer with every second.

Deacon's strength was fading, his grip slipping as the stone ground against his fingers. Panic surged in his chest. With one final wrenching moment of terror, his hand gave way. Gravity claimed him, and he slid helplessly into the dark void below, cold air rushing up to meet him as the world above disappeared.

Chapter 26
Down the Hatch

The world around him spun in a dizzying blur of darkness and chaos as Deacon plummeted down. His fingers scrabbled uselessly against the stone, searching for something—anything—to latch onto. But there was nothing. Just the cold, unyielding rock, and gravity's merciless pull.

Then, suddenly, the freefall stopped. He felt his body slam into a surface, pain flaring up his side as he skidded along what felt like a smooth, slanted wall. He tried to dig in his heels, but the slick moss coating the stone gave no purchase. He was sliding—fast.

The dim light from Hugo's flashlight, which had fallen and lodged itself somewhere above, provided a fleeting glimpse of his surroundings. He was careening down an almost vertical stone chute, the rough walls narrowing as they funneled him downward. Around him, the sound of scraping and thudding filled the tunnel as Sean and Hugo slid down too, their cries mixing with the roar of rushing wind.

"Deacon!" Sean's voice rang out, muffled and distant. Deacon twisted his head, but the momentum kept him hurtling forward.

His breath came in ragged gasps, fear twisting his gut. He had no control—just the cold stone beneath his back and the terrifying speed of their descent.

His mind raced as he hurtled down the slick chute. What if it ended in a sheer drop? What if they plummeted straight into a pit of rocks, or worse? He squinted, trying to make out the path ahead, but it was just a tunnel of darkness. The air grew colder and damper as they were pulled further into the bowels of the island.

And then, with a suddenness that left his heart hammering, the chute ended. Deacon's stomach dropped as he shot out into open space. For a split second, he was weightless, suspended in the air. His arms flailed, his scream echoing off the stone walls, and then—

Splash!

The icy shock of water closed over his head, the force of impact knocking the air from his lungs. He kicked out instinctively, his limbs flailing against the cold, unfamiliar pressure. Bubbles surged around him as he struggled to orient himself, his eyes stinging from the salt.

He broke the surface, gasping, his lungs burning. The world was a blur of dark shapes and crashing waves. "Hugo! Sean!" he choked out, his voice hoarse and desperate.

"Here!" Sean's voice came from somewhere to his left, followed by the sound of splashing. Deacon squinted through the gloom, his eyes finally adjusting enough to see a shadowy figure paddling toward him.

"I'm... I'm here," Hugo called out from behind, his voice strained but steady. Deacon turned and spotted Hugo's head bobbing in the water, his hair plastered to his forehead.

They were in some kind of small sea cave, the walls of the rocky cove rising up steeply around them. It wasn't much more than a notch in the cliff face, but it was enough to give them a moment's respite. The waves, though still strong, were calmer in here, sheltered from the full force of the ocean outside.

"Everyone okay?" Deacon asked, coughing as he tried to catch his breath.

"Define 'okay,'" Sean muttered, rubbing at his shoulder with a wince. "I think I left my stomach back up there somewhere."

Deacon managed a shaky smile despite the fear still pounding in his chest. He glanced around, taking stock of their surroundings. The water was deep, and the walls of the cave curved upward, slick with moss and dripping with moisture. Above them, the mouth of the chute they'd fallen through was barely visible—a dark hole in the rock wall. They wouldn't be climbing back up that way, even if they wanted to. With a tinge of panic, he frantically felt around the outside of his pocket, the comforting bulge of the pendant calming him slightly.

"Where… are we?" Deacon asked, wiping the water from his face.

Hugo turned in a slow circle, scanning the rocky cove. "Some sort of sea cave," he murmured, his brow furrowed in concentration. "Must have been carved out by the tide over the years."

A sound drifted over the water—distant, faint, but unmistakable. The low rumble of a boat engine at idle. Deacon stiffened, his eyes widening.

"Is that…?" Sean began, but Deacon was already paddling toward the opening of the cove, his heart racing. He peered out, blinking against the harsh sunlight that suddenly flooded his vision as he poked his head around the corner.

There, not far from the mouth of the cave, was Captain Jack's boat. It was bobbing in the water, anchored a short distance from the rocks. Relief washed over Deacon, the sight of the old vessel like a lifeline in the storm.

"Jack!" he shouted, waving his arms frantically. "Over here!"

The figure at the helm turned sharply, and a second later, Jack's unmistakable scraggly beard and wide-brimmed hat came into view. He gestured wildly, and the boat's engine roared to life as he guided it toward them.

"What in tarnation are y'all doin' out here?" Jack hollered as he drew closer, his eyes wide with a mix of anger and concern. "I thought you were supposed to be lookin' for that pendant thing, not going for a swim!"

Deacon paddled up to the side of the boat, grabbing onto the railing with one hand. "We found it," he said breathlessly, holding up the pendant. "But we've got company. Remember we told you some bad guys were following us? Well, they're here."

Jack's expression darkened, his mouth setting in a hard line. "I figured as much when I saw that black helicopter drop some fellas off on the top of the island. And I saw several boats closing in a few minutes ago. Looked like they were headin' for the other side of Hawksbill."

"Then we need to go," Hugo said sharply, hauling himself up onto the deck with Jack's help. "Now."

Jack nodded, his eyes flicking warily toward the cliffs rising above them. "Aye. Hold on tight. This is gonna be rough." He shoved the throttle forward, the boat lurching beneath them as it powered away from the cove.

Deacon and Sean scrambled onto the deck, gasping for breath, their clothes clinging to their bodies as icy seawater dripped in steady rivulets. Every muscle in Deacon's body screamed in protest, the strain of the swim and the punishing climb catching up with him now that the adrenaline was fading. Pain radiated from deep bruises and raw scrapes, each one a reminder of their harrowing escape. His limbs felt heavy, trembling with exhaustion, and his chest ached with every breath. He couldn't remember the last time he'd pushed himself this hard. He knew he was nearing his limit, the kind of bone-deep weariness that made him wonder if he could keep going much longer.

Jack maneuvered expertly through the choppy waters, his gaze fixed on the horizon, every muscle in his body tense with concentration. The realization that men had been shooting at them—aimed to kill—finally sank in. A shiver ran down Deacon's spine, a reaction that had nothing to do with the cold water soaking his clothes. His hands shook uncontrollably as his mind replayed those chaotic moments: the deafening gunshots, the splintering rocks, the crumbling ledge. The fear was still there, coiled tightly in his chest, mingling with the faint sense of relief at their narrow escape. But despite the growing distance between them and the chamber filled with Order agents, an oppressive sense of being pursued clung to him like a shadow. He glanced back, his stomach twisting into knots as his eyes caught sight of a sleek, black speedboat slicing through the waves in pursuit, its bow aimed directly at them. The hunt wasn't over. It was just beginning.

"They're coming!" he shouted, pointing to the approaching vessel.

Jack's eyes narrowed, and he cursed under his breath. "Of course they are. Can't a man do a bit of honest piratin' these days without somebody tryin' to horn in on it?"

The speedboat was gaining on them fast, its bow cutting through the water like a knife. Deacon's breath caught in his throat as it drew closer, the figures on board becoming clearer. There were at least three Order agents, all armed, their expressions menacing.

"They're going to catch us!" Sean shouted, gripping the

railing as the boat jolted over a particularly large wave.

"Not if I can help it," Jack muttered. He twisted the wheel hard, veering the boat sharply to the right. The speedboat followed, its engines roaring as it matched their maneuver.

The two vessels tore through the water, each turn bringing them dangerously close to the jagged rocks that jutted up from the sea like teeth. Jack pushed the boat to its limits, but the Order agents were relentless, closing the distance inch by inch.

Then, with a sudden burst of speed, the speedboat surged forward, coming alongside them. One of the agents leaped from their vessel, landing heavily on the deck of Jack's boat. He was tall, broad-shouldered, and looked like he could snap Deacon in half without breaking a sweat.

Deacon staggered back, his heart pounding. The agent's eyes locked onto the pendant clutched in Deacon's hand, a predatory gleam in his gaze.

"Give it to me, boy," the agent growled, his voice low and ominous. "Now."

Deacon's fingers tightened around the pendant as he glanced desperately at Sean and Hugo. They were battered, bruised, and exhausted from the climb and the fall. None of them were in any shape to fight.

He thought of his uncle—a man he'd never known existed but who had sacrificed everything for the tiny pendant now clutched in his trembling hand. He thought of his parents and the lessons they'd imparted: standing up for what's right, no matter how hard it gets. The weight of the pendant seemed to grow heavier with each breath, carrying the hopes of countless people who'd fought to keep it out of the Order's hands. The thought of what the Order would do with this kind of power—the chaos, the manipulation, the sheer destruction— sent a surge of anger and resolve through him. He really had no choice. This wasn't just about protecting the pendant; it was about protecting everything and everyone that mattered. After all, he was a Koster, wasn't he? A watchman. A Guardian.

Squaring his shoulders, Deacon lifted his chin and met the agent's gaze with as much defiance as he could muster. The words that came out felt like a challenge, a vow he intended to keep. "Come and get it."

Chapter 27
Port in the Storm

The salty wind whipped through Deacon's hair as the Order agent lunged, eyes fixed with predatory intensity on the pendant clutched in Deacon's hand. Everything slowed down. The world narrowed to the gleam of determination in the agent's eyes and the glint of his outstretched hand reaching for the pendant.

But just before the agent's fingers could close around it, Hugo's body slammed into the man, knocking him back. Against another man, in another time and place, the blow would have sent him reeling. But here, the weakened Hugo only managed to dislodge the agent a few feet as the two men staggered across the deck, grappling for control. Deacon stumbled back, clutching the pendant to his chest, his heart hammering like a drum. He tried to steady his breath, his thoughts racing as the boat rocked beneath them.

Hugo and the agent circled each other, each testing the other's defenses. Even in his bruised and battered state, Hugo moved with that precision Deacon first noticed back at the cabin; reminiscent of the way his foster-father moved underwater—powerful yet controlled, like a predator circling its prey. But the Order agent was no easy opponent. He was strong, his muscles rippling beneath his soaked clothes as he threw a heavy punch toward Hugo's face.

Hugo ducked and countered with a swift jab to the man's side, but the agent barely flinched, his expression hardening as he swung again, forcing Hugo back a step. The Order operative's movements were aggressive, calculated. Each blow aimed to end the fight swiftly and with brutal efficiency. But Hugo dodged and blocked, pushing back with a skill that seemed effortless despite the exhaustion that lined his face.

"You think you can protect these boys forever?" the agent snarled, driving his shoulder into Hugo's chest, trying to pin him against the railing. Hugo grunted, his body straining against the pressure. He twisted, delivering a sharp elbow to the agent's ribs that sent him reeling. The man stumbled back, and Hugo took the chance to press his advantage, sending a series of rapid strikes into the agent's body.

The man backpedaled, his gaze flicking to Deacon. His lips curled in a sneer, and then—so fast Deacon almost missed it—he produced a wicked looking knife from a sheath on his belt. The knife was long and carbon gray, with a slightly curved tip and a serrated back.

"Watch out!" Sean shouted from behind, but Hugo was already moving.

The agent's knife sliced through the air where Hugo had just been standing. Hugo dodged and grabbed the agent's wrist, twisting it until the blade clattered to the deck. The agent growled in frustration, his fist shooting out and catching Hugo across the jaw. Hugo stumbled, his grip faltering, just as the boat lurched violently to the side.

"Hold on!" Captain Jack yelled from the helm as the boat

banked sharply. Deacon's stomach dropped as the world tilted, and he grabbed the railing with one hand, his other refusing to release the pendant.

The sudden turn threw Hugo off his feet. He hit the deck hard, and before he could recover, the agent was on him. The man's massive hand shot out, wrapping around Hugo's throat like a vice, his other fist cocked back, ready to strike a hammer's blow that would bring the fight to a swift conclusion.

Deacon's eyes widened, the stirrings of panic beginning to surge through him. Without thinking, he snatched up a boat hook lashed below the cabin's windscreen and charged forward. His heart raced, fear and adrenaline mixing in his veins as he swung the hook with all his might.

The metal hook connected with the side of the agent's head with a dull thunk. The man's eyes widened in shock as he staggered, his grip on Hugo loosening. Deacon didn't give him a chance to recover. Grabbing the shaft with both hands, he shoved the boat hook against the agent's chest, driving forward with all the strength remaining in his exhausted legs, using the leverage to push him back—back and over the railing.

With a yell of rage and disbelief, the agent toppled over the side of the boat, hitting the water with a splash. He flailed for a moment before the churning waves and their own boat's forward momentum carried him away.

Deacon stood there, chest heaving, the boat hook still clutched in his trembling hands. He stared at the spot where the agent had vanished, his breath coming in ragged gasps. He barely registered Hugo's hand on his shoulder until the older man squeezed gently.

"You did good, kid," Hugo murmured, his voice low but steady. "Real good."

Deacon nodded numbly, the world spinning around him. He

turned, his gaze catching sight of the Order's speedboat, still closing in fast. His heart skipped a beat as he saw one of the agents raise a rifle, the muzzle glinting ominously in the light.

"Get down!" Hugo shouted, yanking Deacon and Sean down to the deck.

A sharp crack split the air, the sound of a gunshot reverberating over the waves. The bullet whizzed past, missing Deacon's head by inches. His heart pounded in his ears as he glanced up, catching a glimpse of the agent steadying the rifle for another volley of shots.

"We're sitting ducks here!" Sean yelled, his face pale.

Captain Jack's earlier consternation at having someone chase his passengers had turned to rage that someone would dare risk putting a bullet hole in his boat. A steely determination filled his face as he adjusted his grip. "Hold on!" he roared, gripping the wheel with white-knuckled intensity. The boat veered sharply to the left, the hull skimming dangerously close to a jagged outcrop of rocks.

The Order's speedboat followed, the gunman steadying his aim. But just as he lined up his shot, Captain Jack made a daring swerve, steering them between two massive rocks jutting up from the sea like teeth. The maneuver was so sudden, so reckless, that even Deacon's breath caught in his throat.

"Are you crazy?!" Sean screamed, clinging to the railing as the rocks loomed closer.

The boat slid between the rocks with inches to spare, the rough stone scraping against the sides. The Order's speedboat, caught off guard, tried to follow, but it was too late. The bow struck the first rock with a sickening crunch. The speedboat slammed into the rock with a bone-jarring crunch, the fiberglass hull shattering on impact.

Deacon watched, his heart in his throat, as the boat seemed

to explode outward in a shower of splintered fragments. The gunman was thrown off balance, the rifle flying from his hands as the speedboat flipped violently to one side, the remains of the hull grinding against the jagged surface. The engine sputtered, roaring one last time before the twisted remnants of the boat began to sink rapidly, water flooding through the gaping holes torn into the hull.

"Looks like they'll be swimmin' home," Captain Jack muttered, a grim smile tugging at his lips.

Deacon exhaled shakily, sinking to the deck of the boat, the relief washing over him like a wave. He glanced down at the pendant in his hand, the small object that had caused so much chaos, so much danger. Its outline traced red in his palm where he had unknowingly squeezed it so hard during the encounter. It was just a small piece of stone, but it held the power to change everything.

Sean came to sit next to his friend. For once, not saying a word; just sharing the silence as the thrum of the boat's engine lulled their exhausted bodies into the first moment of release they'd had all day.

Hugo stood, pulling his phone from his pocket. He turned away slightly, his voice low as he made the call. "Oliver? Yeah, it's Hugo. Is the transportation I requested still on standby?"

He paused, listening. Deacon noticed Hugo's shoulders stiffen, a look of surprise flickering across his face.

"Wait—who's picking us up?" A few more seconds of silence, and then Hugo's expression tightened, his jaw clenching. "Your nephew? You—no, no… it's fine. I'm sure he's a good driver." A strained smile twisted Hugo's lip. "Yes, sixteen is a… very capable, I'm sure. We'll manage. Thank you."

Hugo ended the call with a deep sigh, shoving the phone back into his pocket. He turned to face Deacon and Sean; his lips pressed into a thin line of irritation.

"Change of plans," Hugo said, his voice tight. "Our ride's still going to be there… but Mr. Oliver thought it'd be a great idea to have his sixteen-year-old nephew pick us up."

Sean blinked, a grin twitching at the corners of his mouth. "Hey, great news, Hugo! You get to make another friend."

Hugo rubbed a hand over his face, the frustration plain in his eyes. "Apparently, the kid just got his license last month. Mr. Oliver thought it would be great practice for him and would save us the money of hiring a local driver. Like that was a concern. But I guess it's either that, or we try to hitchhike out of a tiny North Carolina marina."

"What do we do now?" Deacon asked, feeling the weariness settle deeper into his bones. All he really wanted to do was curl up and sleep for the next twelve hours.

Hugo exhaled deeply. "We get back to the mainland. We play nice with the kid. And we figure out what the Order's next move is before they make ours for us."

Chapter 28
Red Sky at Night

Von Heger stood in the shadows of a nondescript sedan parked at the edge of the marina's lot, his eyes sweeping over the scene with clinical detachment. A gust of briny air blew in from the water, carrying the faint scent of fish and diesel fuel. He glanced at his watch, noting the time with a slight narrowing of his gaze. If his calculations were correct, Deacon Koster and his ragtag group of allies would be here soon.

Patience, patience, he reminded himself. Every setback they had thrown at him thus far was nothing more than a temporary inconvenience. He would see this through. He would recover the pendant and, in doing so, extinguish the last embers of the Koster family's defiance.

A low murmur of conversation crackled through his earpiece. Von Heger's lips curved into the barest hint of a smile as his men relayed their positions across the marina. "Keep your distance," he murmured softly. His voice carried an almost musical cadence, calm and controlled. "We don't want to scare off our guests before the party starts."

He watched with narrowed eyes as a cherry-red Ford Bronco

pulled into the marina's lot, the engine growling softly as it coasted to a stop. The vehicle was far too conspicuous for his tastes—a flash of color in a sea of faded grays and blues. Yet, it fit the nature of the young man who stepped out from behind the wheel.

The boy was tall and lithe with an athletic frame, his tousled blonde hair gleaming in the late afternoon light. Dressed in faded jeans and a button-up flannel shirt rolled to the elbows, he looked utterly out of place amidst the salt-weathered fishermen and their battered pickup trucks. His youth seemed almost comically juxtaposed against the air of cautious wariness that hung over the marina. Leaning casually against the hood of the Bronco, the boy surveyed the water with the nonchalance of someone waiting for friends to arrive for a beach trip, not foraging into the middle of a dangerous game that could end his life.

Von Heger observed him for a moment, his mind whirring as he cataloged every detail. The boy was an anomaly. Too young to be one of Hugo's usual contacts. Too fresh-faced and relaxed for an operative. And yet, the timing of his arrival, the way he lingered by the vehicle as if expecting someone, piqued Von Heger's interest. It was just the sort of coincidence that, in his experience, rarely ended up being a coincidence at all.

"Who are you, then?" he murmured softly, eyes narrowing as he watched the boy drum his fingers absently against the Bronco's door.

Perhaps a relative of one of Hugo's associates? A new recruit, roped into this mess by circumstance? Von Heger dismissed him as a serious threat, but he wasn't foolish enough to ignore any unknown variable. The boy was most likely here to provide a ride for the trio when they returned—an unimportant cog in the greater machine of the Guardians' network.

No matter. He wouldn't be a problem for much longer.

Von Heger reached for his phone and dialed a number with practiced precision. It rang once before a deep voice answered on the other end. "Sir?"

"Listen carefully," Von Heger said, his voice barely more than a whisper, yet carrying the unmistakable weight of command. "I want two of you to head out on route 55. Setup at point Alpha and await activation. That red Bronco in the lot will be the target. You know your role; make sure the welcome party is ready for our friends. I'll make sure the guests arrive myself."

The man on the other end of the line murmured an acknowledgment, and Von Heger ended the call, his gaze still fixed on the boy. He would wait for the Koster boy and his friends to connect with their new driver. And then, when they were out on the open road, away from prying eyes and unplanned interferences, he would make his move.

Von Heger turned slightly, eyes scanning the marina with practiced efficiency. There were a few fishermen milling about near the docks, but none were close enough to overhear anything. A couple of tourists strolled along the water's edge, oblivious to the predator lurking in their midst.

"Tell me, boy," he whispered to himself as he watched the teen peer out toward the horizon, a look of mild impatience crossing his face, "are you ready to meet the devil tonight?"

The thought elicited a small, humorless smile. The marina was no place for a confrontation. Too many unknowns, too many unpredictable variables. But out there, on the empty stretches of backcountry roads that wound through the Carolina coastline, they would have the advantage. No one would hear their cries for help. No one would interrupt.

"Begin phase one," Von Heger ordered softly, pressing his earpiece closer. "Have the perimeter units pull back. We'll intercept them on the outer road leading toward New Bern. I want no mistakes."

"Understood, sir," came the reply, crisp and immediate.

He watched as the agents nearest the marina withdrew, fading into the background like phantoms. Von Heger's eyes never left the boy by the Bronco. He had shifted again, glancing down at his phone and frowning. The boy's movements were restless now, a hint of anxiety seeping through his casual demeanor.

Not as confident as you want to appear, hm? Von Heger thought, amusement glimmering briefly in his cold eyes. No matter. The boy's confidence, or lack thereof, was inconsequential. What mattered was the message Von Heger intended to send.

It was time to show Deacon Koster exactly what it meant to cross paths with the Order. And for Hugo Deroche, it was a reminder of who really pulled the strings in this game they were playing.

Von Heger glanced at his watch again. They would be here soon. The boat should have docked by now. It was unfortunate about the loss of his own boat and men, but such is the price of failure. He let out a slow breath, leaning back against the side of the car as he settled in to wait.

The setting sun painted the sky in brilliant hues of orange and purple, casting long shadows over the marina. It was almost picturesque. Peaceful, even. How did the old saying go? Red sky at night, sailor's delight? He chuckled to himself. There would be no delight tonight for these three. This was merely the calm before the storm.

The Koster boy and his friends had made a habit of slipping through his fingers, but this time would be different. This time, he would be ready for them.

Von Heger glanced at his two closest operatives standing a

few feet away, their eyes sharp and alert. "We'll let them think they've made it out. But once they're on that back road," he said softly, his voice dropping to a dangerous purr, "we'll introduce ourselves properly."

His gaze shifted back to the driver. The boy had straightened, his posture stiffening as he spotted something on the water. A boat, approaching the dock, its silhouette familiar even in the fading light.

Von Heger's smile returned, colder than the wind sweeping in off the water.

"Welcome to the game, Mr. Koster," he murmured. "Let's see how well you play when the stakes are life and death."

Von Heger leaned back against the car, eyes never leaving the teenager by the Bronco. The boy was a temporary complication, an unplanned piece on the board. But if he got in the way, if he proved more troublesome than anticipated… well, Von Heger had dealt with worse. He'd leave the boy out of it for now—he wasn't the one the Order was hunting. Yet.

Von Heger turned his attention back to the water, watching as the boat drew nearer. Failure was a word he despised, but he knew when to cut his losses. The agents lost in the earlier skirmish were already forgotten, buried in the calculations of acceptable cost. Recovering the pendant was all that mattered now. And with Hugo and the boy on the run, the Order's plans had nearly been compromised once before. He wouldn't allow it to happen again. The consequences would be severe if the pendant slipped from his grasp—and those consequences extended far beyond his own position in the Order.

The trap was set, and now it was just a matter of time before the prey walked willingly into its jaws. A twinge of anticipation flared in his chest. Tonight, he would ensure the Koster boy understood just how dangerous it was to defy the Order. He glanced at his operatives. "We'll take them on the road, miles away from any prying eyes. No witnesses." He allowed a thin, humorless smile. "After all, it's a long way back to Ashebridge."

Chapter 29
Bixby

Deacon's eyes strained against the harsh light reflecting off the marina's concrete as he climbed up onto the dock, feeling the ache of every muscle and bruise in his body. He wasn't sure what he'd expected to see after their harrowing escape from Hawksbill Isle, but the sight of a pristine cherry-red Ford Bronco gleaming in the afternoon sun felt almost surreal.

"Over here!" A voice called out, startling Deacon from his thoughts.

He turned to see a tall, blond kid in a flannel shirt and worn jeans leaning casually against the Bronco. The kid's carefree smile seemed out of place, given everything that had just happened. It was like that jarring moment when someone steps out of a dark movie theater into the blinding daylight, blinking as their eyes struggle to adjust. He waved eagerly, pushing off the truck as the group made their way closer.

"Welcome back to the mainland!" the kid called, stepping forward. "You must be Deacon, Sean, and Hugo. I'm Bixby Peters, your ride out of here. Uncle Oliver sent me."

Deacon exchanged a quick glance with Sean and Hugo. After

surviving multiple firefights, a cave-in, and a speedboat chase, this was their ride to safety?

"Uh… yeah," Deacon managed, a little thrown off. "Bixby, right?"

"That's me!" Bixby flashed a grin and gave an exaggerated thumbs up. "Bixby 'Bix' Peters, licensed driver, top of my class in parallel parking, and winner of the Ashebridge High School Second Period Drivers Education Teenage Driver Safety Award." He shot them a cocky smirk as if expecting applause. "So, you guys ready to roll?"

"Teenage driver?" Sean muttered under his breath, nudging Deacon. "Great. Nothing like making our grand getaway in a vehicle driven by someone whose mom still packs their lunch."

Deacon's lips twitched despite the tension coiling in his chest. Sean had a point, but right now, they didn't have much choice. They needed to get off the grid, and this kid was their best shot at blending in.

Hugo stepped forward, his expression tight. "Bixby, thanks for coming out here to get us, but we need to keep moving. Any sign of anyone following you?"

Bixby shook his head, his brow furrowing slightly. "Nope, nada. Just a few fishermen around when I got here. I parked as far back as I could to avoid being too conspicuous, but, uh…" He glanced at the Bronco's brilliant red paint and shrugged sheepishly. "Might have to work on my camouflage game."

Hugo grunted, his gaze flicking to the parking lot. "Right. We'll talk about subtlety later. For now, we need to stay off main roads. Take the back route through the woods, then get us to Raleigh."

Bixby gave a sharp salute, his grin widening. "Aye-aye, captain. Hop in, and let's make this happen."

"Captain?" Sean snorted, rolling his eyes as he headed toward the Bronco. "I think you've been watching too many 'Fast and Furious' movies, Bix."

"Hey, I'm just trying to keep things light!" Bixby defended, holding up his hands. "It's not every day you get a call from your uncle asking you to pick up three mystery people from a secret marina rendezvous. Good thing I was over in Raleigh for football camp already. Otherwise, it would have taken forever to get here coming all the way from Ashebridge."

Sean let out a low whistle, shaking his head. "You're in for a treat, buddy. Just hope you've got good insurance. Things tend to go south when we're involved."

Deacon climbed into the front passenger seat as Hugo settled in the back, his gaze still sweeping the marina. Even now, Hugo's eyes stayed sharp, scanning for any signs of trouble. Deacon felt the familiar tension creeping back in, making his muscles twitch in readiness. They were out of the immediate danger of the island, but they weren't out of the woods yet— figuratively or literally.

The Bronco's engine roared to life with a throaty rumble that seemed out of place in the quiet marina lot. As they pulled out, Deacon twisted in his seat to glance back at the water. The small boat they had escaped on bobbed quietly, anchored and empty, Captain Jack having decided that discretion was the better part of valor. The old man had muttered something about going somewhere far away from his boat and his three recent houseguests. Now, only a silent marina remained, no sign of the Order.

Maybe they really had given them the slip this time.

"So, uh, what exactly did you guys get up to out there?" Bixby asked, glancing at Deacon curiously as he guided the Bronco onto a narrow back road that led away from the coast. "I mean, Uncle Oliver didn't give me any details—just said I was supposed to pick up a few friends of his. I assumed maybe you had been up to some deep-sea fishing, but if so, remind me not to go after whatever you were trying to catch. What happened?"

"Long story," Deacon said, rubbing his sore shoulder absentmindedly. "Let's just say it's been a rough day."

"Rough day, huh?" Bixby grinned, his eyes flicking up to the rearview mirror to catch Sean's gaze. "Sounds like you've got some wild stories to tell. Maybe you can fill me in when we get to Raleigh."

"Yeah, maybe," Sean replied with a weary smile. "If we live that long."

The mood in the car shifted, the lighthearted banter giving way to a heavy silence as the trees blurred by. Bixby drove smoothly, navigating the winding roads with more competence than Deacon would have expected from a kid his age. Maybe he wasn't such a bad choice after all.

Still, Deacon couldn't shake the feeling that something was off. He glanced at Hugo, who had his phone out, his brow furrowed in concentration as he sent a quick text. Deacon caught a glimpse of the screen—a message to someone named V.S., with the words: They've arrived. En route. Status?

"Everything okay?" Deacon asked softly.

Hugo looked up, meeting Deacon's gaze in the rearview mirror. "Just checking in with a friend," he said, his voice neutral. "Making sure all our bases are covered."

"Got it," Deacon murmured, turning back to stare out the window as the Bronco rumbled down the gravel road. His mind buzzed with unease, the hairs on the back of his neck standing on end. He couldn't shake the sensation that they were being watched, followed.

"You okay, man?" Bixby asked, his voice dropping in concern. "You look like you've seen a ghost."

"It's just been one of those days," Deacon replied, his voice tight. He forced himself to take a deep breath, trying to quell the knot of anxiety twisting in his gut. "Just... keep your eyes on the road."

Bixby nodded, his grin fading as he focused on driving. "Roger that. Get some rest. We'll be in Raleigh in a couple hours."

Deacon leaned back in his seat, trying to ignore the growing sense of dread settling over him like a dark cloud. Relax, he told himself. It's just nerves. We're fine. We're getting out of here.

But no matter how many times he repeated it, the feeling wouldn't go away. The Order hadn't given up. They were still out there, somewhere.

And Deacon knew, deep down, that their escape was only temporary. The real danger was still coming.

Chapter 30
Out of the Frying Pan

The Bronco's tires crunched over gravel as Bixby navigated the winding back roads, tall pines and dense underbrush flanking them on either side. The light filtering through the canopy above flickered in staccato bursts, making Deacon feel like they were driving through a tunnel of shadows. He tried to relax, letting the rumble of the engine and the swaying motion of the vehicle lull his overworked mind into a semblance of calm. But he couldn't shake the tension coiled tight in his chest.

Something was wrong.

He glanced back at Hugo, who was staring out the side window, his phone now forgotten in his lap. Even Sean, who usually tried to lighten the mood, was unusually quiet, his gaze flickering nervously around the interior of the vehicle.

"You're sure this route is clear?" Deacon asked, his voice low. He didn't want to sound paranoid, but he'd learned long ago to trust his instincts—and right now, they were screaming at him.

Bixby shrugged, his eyes on the road. "Yeah, man. Hardly anyone uses these roads. It's the long way, but it's the best way to stay under the radar. I come this way with my folks sometimes when we go to the beach and Dad wants to 'avoid the traffic'." He flashed a confident grin. "Besides, no one's following us. We'd know by now, right?"

"Right," Deacon muttered, but his mind was already working through a hundred different scenarios, each worse than the last. The Order wasn't the kind of enemy you could easily lose. They were meticulous, relentless—and if they wanted something, they would move heaven and earth to get it.

And they wanted the pendant. His hand tightened around the small object nestled in his jacket pocket. He could feel its weight, both physical and metaphorical, pressing against him. It was more than just a piece of history. It was power. The kind of power that people would kill for.

"Hey, Hugo?" Bixby's voice broke through Deacon's thoughts, hesitant now. "You didn't say exactly what you guys did to tick these people off, but... are we talking, like, local law enforcement-level trouble or the kind that involves black helicopters and men in black suits?"

Hugo's jaw clenched, his gaze still fixed out the window. "Let's just say it's the kind of trouble that doesn't go away when you leave the county line."

"Cool, cool, cool, cool," Bixby muttered, his knuckles whitening on the steering wheel. "Just pick up some friends of mine, Bixby. You'll get some good driving experience, and I'll pay you thirty bucks plus gas. Thanks a lot, Uncle O."

Deacon almost smiled, but the unease still gnawing at him kept his expression grim. "Just keep driving."

They wound through another series of tight curves, the Bronco's suspension groaning as Bixby navigated the twists and turns. For a while, the silence was broken only by the sound of the tires crunching over loose gravel and the occasional creak of the vehicle's frame.

Then Deacon saw it—a flash of light through the trees. It was quick, barely a glimmer, but it was enough to send his pulse racing.

"Bixby, slow down," he said, his voice sharper than he intended. "Something's up ahead."

"What is it?" Sean asked, his voice tight. He leaned forward, peering through the windshield.

Deacon shook his head, his eyes scanning the trees on either side of the road. There it was again—a brief, bright glint, like sunlight reflecting off glass or metal.

"Stop the car," Hugo ordered suddenly, his voice low but commanding.

Bixby's foot immediately hit the brake, the Bronco coming to a smooth halt in the middle of the road. The silence that followed was deafening, the only sound the faint hum of the engine and the whisper of wind rustling through the pines.

"What is it?" Bixby whispered, his voice barely audible.

Hugo didn't answer. He was already reaching for the door handle, his movements tense and deliberate. "Stay here," he murmured, then slipped out of the vehicle with the silent grace of a predator.

Deacon's breath caught in his throat as he watched Hugo move to the edge of the road, his eyes scanning the trees. He wanted to get out, to do something, but he knew better than to disobey Hugo's orders.

Seconds stretched into what felt like hours as Hugo stood there, perfectly still. Then, without warning, he turned and sprinted back to the Bronco, his expression grim.

"Reverse. Now."

"What? Why?" Bixby asked, confusion and fear mingling in his voice.

"Do it!" Hugo snapped, his voice brooking no argument.

Bixby threw the Bronco into reverse, the tires skidding on the gravel as they backed up. Deacon twisted in his seat, his heart hammering in his chest as he looked out the rear window.

That's when he saw them.

Figures in dark clothing stepped out from behind the trees, emerging like ghosts from the shadows. They moved with practiced precision, rifles slung across their chests, covered by kevlar vests, their faces obscured by masks and tactical helmets.

"Holy Super Banana... go, go, go!" Sean shouted, his voice high with panic.

Bixby stomped on the gas, the Bronco lurching backward with a roar. The Order agents moved swiftly, fanning out across the road, their weapons trained on the vehicle.

Gunfire erupted, the sharp cracks splitting the air as bullets peppered the Bronco's hood, a spiderweb of cracks instantly spreading across the windshield. Bixby cursed, jerking the wheel as he tried to keep the vehicle on the road while reversing at breakneck speed.

"What is going on!?!" he shouted, his voice barely audible over the chaos.

The Bronco skidded backward around a bend, the tires barely gripping the loose gravel. Deacon's heart pounded in his chest as he gripped the seat, his mind racing. They had to get out of here. They had to—

A deafening crash filled the air as the Bronco's rear slammed into something solid. The vehicle shuddered to a halt, the impact jolting through them like a physical blow.

"Everyone okay?" Deacon gasped, his ears ringing.

"Fine, I'm fine," Sean muttered, clutching his shoulder.

Bixby groaned, his head slumping forward. "I—I think we hit something..."

Hugo twisted in his seat, his gaze fierce as he looked around.

"We're boxed in. They've cut us off."

Deacon's stomach dropped as he realized the truth of Hugo's words. More figures were emerging from the trees, surrounding the Bronco. There was no way out.

"What do we do?" Bixby whispered, his voice trembling.

Hugo's jaw tightened, his gaze locking onto Deacon's. "Give me the pendant."

"What?" Deacon's voice came out strangled, his hand instinctively covering his pocket.

"Trust me," Hugo said, his voice low and urgent. "It's the only way we have a chance to walk out of here alive. You have to let it go."

The weight of the pendant seemed to increase as Deacon's fingers tightened around it. Every instinct screamed at him to run, to protect it. But Hugo's eyes were steady, filled with a grim determination that left no room for doubt.

With a sinking feeling, Deacon reached into his pocket and pulled out the pendant, its surface cool and smooth against his skin. He handed it over, his fingers trembling. It felt wrong to give it up after everything they had gone through to get it. But what other choice did they have?

Hugo took the pendant and slipped it into a small leather pouch at his waist, his movements precise. Then he looked at Deacon and Sean, his expression hard. "Stay in the car. No matter what happens, do not get out. Let me handle this."

"What are you going to do?" Sean asked, his voice tight with fear.

Hugo's face was grim. "Whatever I can."

He opened the door and stepped out, raising his hands slowly. The Order agents closed in, their weapons trained on him.

"Hold your fire!" a commanding voice called out, and the agents froze, their rifles lowering slightly.

A man stepped forward, his gaze sweeping over Hugo with cold amusement. "Ah, Mr. Deroche. I see you've finally decided to surrender. How very… practical of you."

The speaker was of average height, but powerfully built. Coal black hair silvering at the temples framed sharp cheeks and dark eyes that commanded authority. The fading light shimmered off a silver brooch adorning his vest; a stag overlaid on a V-shaped shield. The same symbol left for them in Jamaica. Deacon realized this must be Von Heger.

Von Heger's gaze shifted from Hugo to the Bronco, and then lingered on Deacon and Sean, assessing them with a calculating intensity. Finally, he turned his full attention back to Hugo, his smile widening. "I must admit, I expected more of a chase from you, Hugo. But I suppose even the mighty Deroche knows when he's outmatched."

"Cut the theatrics, Von Heger," Hugo growled, his voice low and tense. "You want the pendant? Fine. Take it and leave the boy alone."

Von Heger's eyes glittered with cold amusement. "Ah, so protective of the young Koster. You always did have a soft spot for that family. But this isn't just about the pendant, is it?" He took a step closer, his gaze piercing. "You know what it means for us to have it. You know what it could do if used correctly."

Hugo didn't flinch, but Deacon saw a flicker of something—fear, anger, maybe both—cross his face. "I know what you're capable of, Von Heger. That's why I'm here."

"Then hand it over," Von Heger purred, extending a gloved hand. "And perhaps I'll let you all live to see another day."

Hugo glanced at the pouch on his belt, his jaw clenched tight. Slowly, he unhooked it and held it out, the leather strap dangling from his fingers. The air was thick with tension, every breath charged with anticipation.

Von Heger's gaze flicked to the pendant pouch, his smile widening. "There's a good boy."

Before Hugo could react, one of the Order agents stepped forward, ripping the pouch from his grasp. The agent retreated quickly, handing the pouch to Von Heger.

Von Heger's fingers curled around the pouch, his expression triumphant as he carefully drew out the pendant. He held it up to the light, examining it with a meticulous eye.

Deacon's heart sank as he watched the pendant's surface catch the light, its etched symbols gleaming faintly. It was Eshu's Pendant. The one they had fought so hard to retrieve. The thing they'd risked so much for over the last few days. And now it was in the hands of their enemy.

Von Heger's gaze shifted to Deacon, his eyes narrowing slightly. He turned the pendant slowly in his hand, as if weighing it, then let out a soft, thoughtful hum. "So, this is what all the fuss is about," he murmured, his gaze locking onto Deacon's. "You must be the Koster boy. The one who managed to evade us at every turn."

Deacon swallowed hard, but he held Von Heger's gaze, refusing to show fear. "Give it back," he said, his voice steady despite the thundering of his heart.

Von Heger chuckled softly, the sound almost fatherly. "Such spirit. I can see why you've been such a thorn in our side. So much like your uncle." He glanced at Hugo, his smile turning condescending. "I suppose I should commend you, Hugo, for keeping him alive this long. But you've only delayed the inevitable. You know I'll have to do to him the same as I did to his weak uncle." This last line delivered as Von Heger turned to stare into Deacon's eyes.

"Take the pendant and go, Von Heger," Hugo said, his voice hard. "You have what you want."

Von Heger raised an eyebrow, his smile widening. "You misunderstand, Hugo. This isn't just about possession. It's about control. Power. And ensuring that young Deacon here knows exactly who holds it."

He stepped closer to the Bronco, his gaze still locked on Deacon. "Tell me, boy. Do you know what this pendant is capable of?"

Deacon's breath hitched, but he forced himself to answer. "It's… it's supposed to influence people, make them believe things that aren't real."

"Very good," Von Heger murmured approvingly. "But that's just the beginning. This pendant can shape reality itself. The mind is a powerful tool, and with the right influence… it can be twisted, molded to see whatever I want it to see."

He leaned in, his gaze boring into Deacon's. "Imagine, young Koster, if I told you that you were my ally. That your friends were your enemies. That the world outside this car was nothing but an illusion. What would you believe then?"

"Stop it," Deacon whispered, his chest tightening. "Just… stop."

Von Heger chuckled, a low, menacing sound. "Don't worry. I won't use it on you. Not yet, anyway. You've proven to be an interesting adversary. It would be a shame to break you so soon."

He straightened, his expression hardening. "Take them."

The Order agents moved in, guns trained on the Bronco as they surrounded the vehicle. Hugo stood his ground, his fists clenched at his sides.

Von Heger's gaze shifted to Hugo, his smile fading. "If you value their lives, Deroche, you'll cooperate. Any resistance, and I won't hesitate to use this." He held the pendant up, its surface gleaming ominously in the fading light.

"Understood?" he asked softly.

Hugo nodded stiffly, his gaze never leaving Von Heger's face. "I understand you perfectly."

Von Heger nodded once, satisfied. "Good. Now, let's get moving. We have much to discuss."

The Order agents closed in, and Deacon felt a surge of helplessness wash over him. The pendant was gone. Von Heger had it. And now they were at his mercy.

There was no escape. Not this time.

Von Heger turned away, pocketing the pendant with a final, triumphant smile. "Welcome to the game, Mr. Koster. I do hope you enjoy playing."

The sound of approaching vehicles filled the air, the low hum of engines mingling with the rustle of leaves and the distant cawing of birds.

Their fate, it seemed, was sealed.

The game was far from over. But this time, the Order held all the cards.

Chapter 31
The Cavalry

Von Heger's smile widened as he turned his gaze back to Hugo. The pendant dangled from his fingers, the faint gleam of the setting sun casting eerie shadows across its etched surface. He rolled it between his fingers, savoring the victory.

"Tell me, Mr. Deroche," he murmured, his voice a low purr, "what will the Guardians do without you? Without the boy? That will be the end of the Koster family. Quite the blow to such a storied organization, no?"

Hugo clenched his jaw, his gaze never wavering from the pendant. "You don't know the Guardians as well as you think, Von Heger. Cut off one head, and two more take its place."

"Ah, the classic Hydra analogy. But as you can see—" Von Heger raised the pendant higher, letting it catch the last rays of light. "—I've already severed the head. The rest of you are just waiting to be crushed underfoot."

Deacon's breath hitched, the weight of their situation pressing down on him like a vise. Two agents roughly pulled him out of the Bronco while others moved in, guns raised, fingers tense on the triggers. The urge to run, to do something, surged through him, but Hugo's presence beside him was like an anchor, keeping him grounded.

"Take them," Von Heger ordered, his voice dripping with satisfaction. "It's time we ended this charade."

But before the agents could follow his order, the distant hum of an engine filled the air. Von Heger frowned, his gaze shifting toward the curve in the road behind the Bronco. Deacon's heart skipped a beat as a pair of headlights cut through the growing darkness, the vehicle's beams illuminating the dusty road.

The agents hesitated, their movements faltering as the car's headlights bore down on them. Von Heger's eyes narrowed, his expression darkening as the sleek black SUV screeched to a halt a few yards away. The engine thrummed, idling with a steady, menacing purr.

The driver's door swung open, and a tall figure stepped out. A woman. She moved with the easy confidence of someone used to command, her posture relaxed but radiating a dangerous energy that seemed to crackle in the air around her. Deacon blinked, trying to take in the unexpected presence before them.

She was striking—light chocolate skin, long legs accentuated by black combat boots, and wavy black hair pulled back in a low ponytail. Her eyes, a piercing green that seemed almost unnatural in their intensity, swept over the scene with cool precision. She wore a tailored black jacket over a simple white shirt and dark cargo pants, the only visible weapons a sleek handgun strapped to her thigh and a compact rifle slung across her back.

"Good evening, gentlemen," she said, her voice calm and measured, with just the faintest hint of an accent that Deacon couldn't quite place. Her gaze shifted to Von Heger, and something sharp and dangerous flashed in her eyes. "Terribly rude of me to show up without an invention, I know."

Von Heger's face hardened. "Ms. Odeku," he said softly, his tone betraying a flicker of annoyance. "I see the Guardians are sending their lapdogs to sniff around after all. Did they really think you'd be enough to handle this?"

Delilah's lips twitched in a faint smile, her eyes never leaving Von Heger's face. "Oh, I'm not here on their orders, if that's what you're thinking. You know I prefer to do things my way."

She took a step closer, the rifle shifting slightly on her back, and Deacon felt his pulse quicken. Every move she made was deliberate, controlled. Even standing still, she looked like she was ready to spring into action at any second. "Hello, Hugo," she purred, never taking her eyes off Von Heger.

"Um, hey there, Delilah," Hugo managed in a voice somewhere between nervous and irritated.

Von Heger raised an eyebrow, his gaze sweeping over Delilah with thinly veiled disdain. "This is none of your concern, Odeku. I suggest you walk away before you get hurt."

Delilah's smile widened slightly. "Now, you know I can't do that, Von Heger. You have something that doesn't belong to you." Her eyes flicked to the pendant in his hand. "And I'm afraid I'll have to take it back."

The agents tightened their grips on their weapons, eyes darting between Von Heger and Delilah. A tense silence settled over the clearing, the air thick with anticipation.

Von Heger's fingers tightened around the pendant, his gaze locking onto Delilah's. "You're outnumbered and outgunned. I don't know what game you're playing, but you won't be leaving here with the pendant."

"Outnumbered?" Delilah tilted her head, her smile widening just a fraction. "Perhaps. But I know your men, Von Heger, and I like my odds."

Before Von Heger could respond, Delilah's hand blurred

toward her hip. A flash of movement—a small, metallic canister arced through the air, landing at the feet of the nearest Order agents. Deacon barely had time to register what was happening before a blinding flash exploded outward, followed by a concussive bang that shook the air.

Deacon ducked, squeezing his eyes shut against the searing light. Shouts and curses erupted around them, the Order agents stumbling back, disoriented by the sudden burst. When he blinked his eyes open, he saw Delilah moving—no, gliding—through the chaos, her rifle snapping up as she fired off a series of precise shots. —*Pop-pop-pop!*

Three agents went down, their weapons clattering to the ground. Delilah moved with the fluid grace of a dancer, every shot deliberate and controlled. She advanced on Von Heger, who stood his ground, his expression a mask of cold fury.

"Fall back!" Von Heger barked, his voice cutting through the confusion. "Regroup!"

The remaining agents scrambled, their movements sluggish as they tried to regain their bearings. Delilah didn't let up. She fired again, forcing them to retreat even further, the agents ducking behind trees and rocks for cover.

Hugo was already moving, his hand grabbing Deacon's shoulder. "Get out, now!" he shouted, his voice urgent. "Into the woods!"

"Go!" Delilah called over her shoulder, her voice sharp but steady. "I'll cover you!"

Deacon didn't need to be told twice. He grabbed Sean's arm, pulling him out of the Bronco, and they stumbled toward the tree line. Bixby hesitated, his eyes wide with shock as he stared at the unfolding chaos.

"Bixby!" Hugo barked. "Move!"

That snapped him out of his daze. With a strangled curse,

Bixby threw open the driver's door and bolted after Deacon and Sean, the three of them crashing through the underbrush. Behind them, gunfire echoed through the woods, Delilah's shots interspersed with the crack of returning fire from the Order agents.

"Hugo!" Deacon shouted, glancing back just in time to see Hugo dive into the cover of the trees, his own pistol drawn and firing at the pursuing agents.

"Keep going!" Hugo yelled, his voice carrying through the darkening woods. "Don't stop!"

Deacon turned and ran, his breath coming in harsh gasps as branches whipped at his face and tangled around his legs. He could hear Sean panting beside him, Bixby's footsteps thundering behind them. *—Bang! Bang!*

Gunshots cracked through the air, closer now. The agents were regrouping, recovering from the flashbang. Deacon pushed himself harder, adrenaline driving him forward.

They reached a small clearing, the underbrush giving way to a patch of open ground. Deacon skidded to a stop, his chest heaving as he looked around, heart racing. "Where's Hugo?"

"I'm here," Hugo's voice came from behind a clump of trees. He emerged, his face slick with sweat, his gaze darting around the clearing. "We need to keep moving. Delilah's buying us time, but it won't last."

"Who is she?" Sean asked breathlessly. "She just—she took them on by herself!"

Hugo's expression tightened, a mix of emotions flashing across his face—relief, anger, something else Deacon couldn't quite place. "An old...friend," he said shortly. "Now move. We're not out of this yet."

They plunged back into the trees, the sounds of gunfire and shouts fading behind them. Deacon's thoughts whirled as they ran. Whoever Delilah Odeku was, and it did seem like there was some interesting history there between her and Hugo, she'd just given them a fighting chance.

But as they fled deeper into the woods, one thought nagged at the back of his mind.

She hadn't come to rescue them on Hugo's orders. So, who had sent her? And what else did she know about the pendant that Hugo hadn't told them?

There was no time to think about it now. All that mattered was staying alive long enough to figure it out.

"Keep moving!" Hugo urged, his voice low and urgent. "We need to reach the road. We'll circle back, get to Delilah's car. With any luck, she'll be able to hold them off until then."

Deacon nodded, his muscles burning as he pushed himself forward. The pendant was gone, taken by Von Heger. But they still had each other—and they weren't about to give up now.

Not by a long shot.

Chapter 32
The Plan

The trees seemed to close in around them as the group navigated through the dense underbrush, their footfalls muffled by the soft carpet of pine needles and fallen leaves. Each step was an effort, the exhaustion of the day's events weighing on their limbs. It felt like they'd been running forever, their pursuers always one step behind. But finally, after what felt like an eternity, the small clearing where Delilah's vehicle was parked came into view.

The SUV's sleek, dark shape loomed in the shadows, a stark contrast to the wild, unruly nature surrounding it. The headlights were off, but the engine emitted a faint, steady hum, like a predator lying in wait. Delilah stood beside the driver's side, her posture relaxed yet alert, as if she were expecting them all along.

"Finally, there you are," she remarked, her voice carrying the refined lilt of West End London but softened just enough to sound almost conversational. "I was beginning to wonder if you lot had decided to make camp out there for the night."

Hugo, still catching his breath, gave her a flat look. "Had to take a slight detour. Didn't want to run back into your friend, Von Heger."

Her lips quirked up in a half-smile. "He certainly does have a knack for making his presence felt, doesn't he?" Her gaze shifted to Deacon and Sean, who were leaning heavily against a tree, their faces drawn with fatigue. "The famous young Koster and his loyal companion. I must say, you've caused quite a stir. I can see why Von Heger is so aggravated by the two of you."

Deacon straightened, brushing a hand through his hair, still trying to shake off the lingering adrenaline. "Aggravated? From that reception he just gave us, I'd say that's putting it mildly."

A soft chuckle escaped Delilah's lips as she turned to take in the last member of their party, her eyebrow arching slightly at the sight of Bixby. He stood a few feet away, eyes narrowed, and arms crossed over his chest. The fierce glare in his eyes would have been more intimidating if his lower lip hadn't been trembling ever so slightly with suppressed frustration.

"And you must be… Bixby, correct?" Delilah inquired, her voice dropping a note as if she were considering something carefully. "I'm sorry, but I don't recall you being part of the operation."

Bixby's shoulders squared, his gaze defiant. "I'm not part of anything. I was just supposed to give these guys a ride. And now my Bronco is smashed to pieces thanks to you and your what, secret organization?!" He stepped closer, his voice rising. "What are you, some kind of spy ring? Is this what you people do? Put innocent bystanders in danger?"

Deacon winced, exchanging a quick glance with Sean. Bixby's anger wasn't entirely unwarranted, but they couldn't afford for him to go storming off right now. Not when they still needed his help.

"Not spies, but we are part of a secret organization," Delilah acknowledged coolly, though there was a hint of sympathy in her eyes. "But believe me, Bixby, your involvement was completely unintentional. We will take you to Raleigh and get you a ride home right away."

"Are you kidding me?" Bixby snapped. "Did you see what they did to my truck? I'm not going anywhere. Not until I've helped take down the people who did this."

Hugo let out a low sigh, muttering something under his breath. But Delilah didn't seem put off by Bixby's bravado. Instead, she nodded thoughtfully, her gaze appraising him in a way that made Deacon feel like she was looking right through him.

"This is much bigger than your Bronco, Bixby. But I understand your anger. Very well," she said finally. "You may stay, but on one condition—you follow my orders, and you don't take unnecessary risks. This isn't a game. People can get hurt."

"Yeah, I got that part," Bixby muttered, his shoulders slumping slightly. He glanced over at Deacon, some of the fire leaving his eyes. "I just want to help."

"We know," Deacon said softly. "And we're glad you're here."

Delilah gave a small nod of approval before gesturing toward the SUV. "Now, why don't we get out of here before Von Heger's minions decide to pay us another visit? We can continue this conversation in a safer location."

As they made their way to the vehicle, Bixby's gaze lingered on the sleek lines of the SUV. He let out a long, low whistle, shaking his head. "Nice ride. Not exactly what I'd expect for someone working in the shadows."

Delilah's eyes sparkled with a hint of amusement. "Appearances can be deceiving, Bixby. You'll learn that quickly enough."

They climbed into the SUV, Delilah taking the driver's seat

and Hugo beside her. Sean, Deacon, and Bixby squeezed into the back, the tight quarters making for an awkward silence that none of them seemed eager to break.

After thirty minutes driving over rough forest service roads, the group arrived at their destination and were greeted by a cabin nestled in the heart of the reserve. From the outside, it looked like a typical rustic retreat—wooden walls, a stone chimney, patches of moss growing near the foundation and a wide front porch that creaked underfoot. But the moment Delilah opened the door and flipped a switch, the interior was flooded with light, revealing a space that looked more like a command center than a woodland getaway.

Monitors lined one wall, displaying multiple camera feeds from around the property. A large table dominated the center of the room, strewn with blueprints and tactical gear. Weapons of various makes and models hung neatly on a reinforced steel rack, and a series of sleek black cases, marked with symbols that Deacon didn't recognize, were stacked in one corner.

Sean let out a low whistle, his eyes wide as he took in the scene. "Wow, imagine the VRBO listing description for this place."

Delilah arched an eyebrow, a ghost of a smile playing on her lips. "I do try to keep it comfortable. Please, make yourselves at home and I hope you'll leave me a five-star review."

They settled around the table, the tension from the car ride beginning to dissipate in the face of their surroundings. Delilah moved to one of the monitors and pulled up a detailed map of the Raleigh-Durham area, several red dots marking key locations.

"Now that we're all here," she began, "let's review the situation. Intelligence indicates Von Heger is likely taking the pendant to an Order-controlled research facility in the Raleigh-

Durham area. It's a high-security installation, well-guarded and with limited access. They'll most likely conduct tests and move it through their network of operatives before sending it to one

of their more fortified bases in Europe."

"Which means we have to move quickly if we want to get it back," Hugo added, his tone grim. "Once it's gone, it'll be nearly impossible to track."

"So, we're just supposed to go in there and steal it back?" Sean asked, raising an eyebrow. "Kind of a big ask, don't you think?"

Delilah nodded slowly. "Absolutely. Which is why we need to figure out exactly how we're going to do it. I'm not suggesting we storm the place guns blazing. That would be suicide."

"Then what's the plan?" Deacon asked, leaning forward, his brow furrowing. "You know more about this than we do. What's our next move?"

Delilah's gaze flickered toward Hugo for a split second before returning to the group. "First, we need to understand what we're dealing with. This pendant—Eshu's Pendant—isn't just any artifact. It's linked to Eshu, the Yoruba deity known as the trickster god. Eshu is the guardian of the crossroads, the mediator between worlds, the one who decides whether travelers meet fortune or ruin."

She paused, letting the weight of her words settle over them. "The pendant holds a fraction of that power. It's said to be able to influence people's perceptions, to make them see that which isn't there. That's why Von Heger wants it. In the wrong hands, it could be used to control or manipulate others on a massive scale."

"We sure could use a little of that trickery ourselves," Sean said, leaning back in his chair and crossing his arms. "Give them a taste of their own medicine."

Delilah paused, studying him thoughtfully. "Yes, Sean, precisely. But we have to be careful. If we go in with a half-baked plan, we'll be playing right into Von Heger's hands."

"Then we make a good one," Deacon said firmly. He looked around the table, determination hardening his voice. "We can do this. We just need to be smarter, faster, and a little bit lucky."

A flicker of a smile crossed Delilah's face, her eyes glinting with a hint of approval. "Then let's get to work."

She spread the blueprints out on the table, and the group leaned in, studying every detail, every potential weak point.

Hours passed, ideas were debated, and plans were drawn. When they finally reached a consensus, they had something that, with a titanic-sized amount of luck, just might work.

Delilah leaned back, arms crossed, as she surveyed the blueprint. "We've got the framework. But there's one problem— no one's getting into that facility without the proper credentials. We either must steal a badge, which is nearly impossible given the timeframe, or we need a way to create our own entry point in their system. So, unless one of you happens to be a world-class hacker—"

Deacon's face lit up with sudden inspiration. "I know someone who can help with that."

The others turned to look at him, surprise and curiosity mingling in their gazes. Delilah tilted her head slightly. "Someone who can get us into the Order's security system? That's a tall order, Deacon."

A smile tugged at the corners of Deacon's lips as he nodded. "Trust me. If anyone can do it, it's her."

Chapter 33
And They're Off

The faint glow of monitors cast eerie shadows across the walls of the safehouse basement, creating an atmosphere of tension and anticipation. The room buzzed with low conversations and the soft hum of equipment as the team prepared for the mission ahead. Blueprints of the Order's research facility were spread out on a large table, surrounded by a mess of cables, tactical gear, and half-empty coffee cups.

Deacon's eyes swept over the intricate lines of the blueprint once more, tracing the security checkpoints and restricted areas. His heart thudded in his chest as he committed each turn, each corridor, to memory. He knew they were well-prepared, but that didn't ease the knot of anxiety twisting in his stomach.

"This is it," Delilah said, her voice calm but edged with intensity. She stood at the head of the table, her gaze sweeping over the group. "Last review before we head out. Everyone knows their roles?"

Sean, leaning against the wall with his arms crossed, raised a hand lazily. "Yeah, yeah. Deacon and I are the eye candy. Hugo's the muscle. You're the mastermind, and Bixby's... comic relief, I guess?" He shot a grin at Bixby, who was fidgeting in his seat, his knee bouncing up and down like a jackhammer.

Bixby scowled. "I'm the wheelman. I'm not letting anyone near that SUV if I can help it."

"Exactly," Delilah said, a faint smile tugging at her lips. "And Maria will be our eyes and ears, making sure we can get in and out without tripping any alarms. Hugo, you'll plant the sensor device in the containment area and create a diversion. Deacon and Sean will act as lookouts and help ensure the guards are kept busy."

Deacon nodded, his fingers brushing against the pocket of his jacket where he kept a small earpiece and micro-radio transmitter—both courtesy of the Guardian's inventory of tech gadgets. "We only get one shot at this," he murmured, half to himself. "If Von Heger figures out what we're doing…"

"He won't," Delilah interjected, her voice firm. "He's too focused on outmaneuvering us. He thinks he's already a step ahead." She paused, her gaze flicking to Hugo, who stood by the door, arms folded across his chest. "You're ready?"

Hugo gave a short nod, his expression unreadable. "Let's just get it done."

Delilah's gaze lingered on him for a moment longer before she turned back to the others. "Remember, the pendant is just a symbol. The real power here is in who controls the narrative. Von Heger is arrogant. He thinks he can predict every move we make, which means he's going to try to control the situation. Our job is to make him think he's winning."

"Let's hope he's as overconfident as you think," Deacon muttered.

"Confidence has never been in short supply in that family," Delilah said softly. "Trust me."

A brief silence fell over the room, filled only by the soft

clicking of Maria's keyboard heard over the speakerphone as she sat more than 1,000 miles to south, back in Montego Bay. "Alright, I've got you all logged in as temporary contractors. It'll give you access through the first two levels of security, but once you're past that, you're on your own. I've set a timer for fifteen minutes. That's how long the credentials will hold before the system boots you out."

"Fifteen minutes?" Sean whistled low. "Easy peasy."

Deacon's pulse quickened. They'd have to move fast. There wouldn't be any room for mistakes.

"Just stay calm and stick to the plan," Delilah said, her voice cutting through the tension. "We'll be monitoring you from here the whole time. If anything goes wrong, we pull you out immediately."

"Let's hope it doesn't come to that," Hugo grunted.

Delilah's eyes softened for a brief second. "Stay safe, everyone. And remember, the objective isn't to take the pendant right away. It's to get Von Heger to move it."

"And we'll be right behind them when they do," Deacon added, his voice gaining strength as the plan crystallized in his mind. "Ready, Sean?"

"Born ready," Sean replied, pushing off the wall with a grin. "Let's go jewelry shopping."

Order Research Facility – Raleigh-Durham, NC

Delilah adjusted her position in the surveillance van parked several blocks from the facility's entrance, her eyes glued to the live feeds streaming in from various angles around the compound. She tapped a small earpiece, tuning in to the radio frequency connecting her to the rest of the team.

"Team One, check-in," she murmured.

"Team One, in position," Hugo's voice crackled back, low and steady.

"Team Two?"

"Ready to rock and roll," Sean replied, his tone casual but laced with a hint of nerves.

Delilah smiled faintly, her gaze flitting to the screen displaying a thermal readout of the building. "Everything looks clear on my end. You have a green light. Proceed as planned."

She watched as three heat signatures moved cautiously through the facility's perimeter, their outlines ghostly against the backdrop of the building's warm, glowing core. The first checkpoint passed without issue, then the second. Her heart hammered in her chest as they approached the third, more heavily guarded entrance.

"Stop," Delilah whispered sharply. The figures froze. "There's movement—third door to your left."

On the screen, a guard shifted position, glancing down the hallway before turning and walking away. Delilah let out a breath she hadn't realized she was holding.

"Clear," she murmured. "Go."

The team slipped through the door and into the inner corridors of the facility. Delilah's pulse quickened. This was it—the moment where everything could fall apart or come together perfectly.

"Stay sharp," she whispered, more to herself than to the team. "You're almost there."

The interior of the Order's research facility was a maze of sterile hallways and glass-walled laboratories, each room filled with high-tech equipment and guarded by thick metal doors. Deacon moved carefully, keeping close to Hugo as they made their way down a long corridor, every muscle in his body coiled tight with tension.

"Containment chamber up ahead," Hugo murmured,

nodding toward a heavy, steel-reinforced door at the end of the hallway. A digital panel glowed faintly beside it, indicating the presence of multiple security layers.

Deacon glanced at his watch. They had less than five minutes before their temporary credentials expired.

"Let's move," he whispered.

Hugo stepped forward, punching in the access code that Maria had provided. The panel beeped, and a small green light flashed. The door slid open with a soft hiss, revealing a small, dark room lined with shelves of artifacts and objects, each one more bizarre and arcane than the last.

And there, in the center of the room, suspended in a glass case, was the pendant.

Eshu's Pendant.

Even through the glass, Deacon could feel its pull—a strange, unsettling sensation that seemed to tug at the edges of his consciousness. He swallowed hard, his eyes locked on the small, seemingly unremarkable object that had caused so much chaos in their lives.

"Okay, plant the device," Hugo ordered, his voice low and urgent.

Deacon moved to the far corner of the room, slipping the small, black sensor out of his pocket and attaching it to the underside of a metal shelf. The device emitted a faint red glow before going dark.

"It's done," Deacon whispered.

"Good," Hugo replied. He pulled out a small cylindrical object—a smoke canister, modified to release a thin, odorless gas that would set off the facility's fire suppression systems without causing real damage.

Hugo twisted the cap, and a soft hiss filled the air. "Let's get out of here."

They turned and headed back toward the door, hearts pounding in unison. Behind them, the canister released its contents, and the alarm system began to beep softly.

"Fire alarm activated," Delilah's voice crackled in Deacon's earpiece. "Von Heger will get the alert any second now."

As Deacon and Hugo made their way back down the corridor, Deacon's pulse thrummed with a mix of exhilaration and nerves. Just a little further, and they'd be out of the containment wing. The faint sound of their footsteps echoed softly off the sterile walls, a stark contrast to the chaotic alarms that had begun to blare.

The canister had done its job—now they needed to make their exit.

But then a second, louder alarm roared to life, cutting through the facility like a blade. Deacon froze, glancing sharply at Hugo. This alarm was different, more urgent. They hadn't planned for this.

"What is that?" Deacon whispered, his heart hammering in his chest.

"Security override," Hugo muttered, his eyes narrowing as he scanned the hallway. "Von Heger must have triggered it."

Deacon's stomach churned as Von Heger's voice came over the facility's loudspeakers, sharp and commanding. "All units, lock down the containment chamber! Secure the artifact and prepare for immediate transport. Unauthorized personnel have breached the facility."

A shiver ran down Deacon's spine. They'd been found out—at least partially.

"Keep moving!" Hugo hissed, his voice fierce. "Don't look back."

Deacon swallowed hard and pushed forward, his mind racing. The alarms, the lockdown… It was exactly what they wanted to happen. It meant Von Heger believed their ruse. He was moving the pendant—making it vulnerable.

But that didn't make it any less terrifying.

"Delilah," Hugo growled into his earpiece, his voice low and tense. "We need to know what they're doing."

Delilah's voice crackled back, calm despite the urgency in her tone. "They're mobilizing, just as we thought. Stay on course. You're almost clear."

Deacon took a deep breath and forced himself to focus. This was only the first step. They needed to stay sharp if they were going to see this through.

The real heist was just beginning.

Chapter 34
Cross-Check

Surveillance Room, Order's Facility

Von Heger stood in the center of the surveillance room, hands clasped behind his back. His eyes, sharp and unblinking, were fixed on the array of monitors lining the wall before him. He watched Deacon's team move through the facility, their movements deliberate yet cautious. The faintest smile curled his lips as the fire alarm blared through the speakers—a sound he'd been expecting.

"Just where I want you," he murmured softly.

The room buzzed with quiet activity. Agents manned consoles, typing rapidly as they monitored different sections of the building. The occasional murmur of conversation filled the air, but Von Heger didn't hear any of it. His attention was wholly focused on the trio on the screen.

He reached for the intercom and pressed a button. "Status report."

An agent nearby turned, a tablet clutched in his hands. "The fire alarm has been triggered, sir. The intruders are moving toward Sector B, but so far, they haven't set off the high-security protocols. Containment chamber is still secure."

"Of course it is," Von Heger replied smoothly, his tone almost dismissive. "They'll head there next. Just like we planned."

The agent hesitated. "But if they breach—"

"They won't," Von Heger interrupted, his voice firm. "Not the real containment chamber, at least."

Before the agent could respond, another alert flashed across one of the screens—bright red text accompanied by a sharp alarm. Von Heger's eyes narrowed as he scanned the message: **Containment Breach Detected. Duplicate Artifact Found**.

He allowed himself a quiet chuckle, shaking his head slowly. "Ah, the Guardians. Hundreds of years to hone their craft and they still continually underestimate their opponent."

"Shall I send a team to intercept?" the agent asked, his voice wavering slightly.

Von Heger waved a dismissive hand. "No need. We knew they'd try something like this. Retrieve the real pendant and prepare for transport. I want it out of here within the hour."

"Yes, sir." The agent hurried off, barking orders into his earpiece.

Von Heger turned back to the monitors, his smile widening. "You think you've fooled me, don't you, Hugo?" he murmured softly. "But you're not nearly as clever as you imagine."

He watched as the trio slipped past another set of guards, their movements confident and precise. For a moment, he almost admired their audacity. Almost.

"Continue moving your pieces around the board," he whispered, his gaze shifting to the screen displaying a view of the containment chamber. "Because soon, you'll find out just how little control of the game you actually have."

Deacon flattened himself against the cool, metallic wall of the hallway, the incessant blare of the fire alarm ringing in his ears. His heart pounded as he glanced around, scanning for any signs of the guards that might be on their tail.

"Almost there," Sean whispered, his voice barely audible above the alarm.

Deacon nodded, gripping the small handheld device in his pocket. A few taps, and the tiny screen flickered to life, displaying a series of encrypted codes. "Maria's got us access through the next checkpoint. We've got maybe five minutes before the system catches on."

Hugo, standing a few steps ahead, glanced over his shoulder. "We move now."

They crept forward, keeping to the shadows. The containment chamber was just up ahead—a heavy, reinforced door flanked by security cameras and a digital keypad. The fire alarm was still going, but no other alerts had been triggered yet. They needed to move fast.

"Delilah," Hugo murmured into his earpiece, his voice low but steady. "We're in position. Begin phase two."

A soft crackle of static, then Delilah's calm voice came through. "Copy that. Stand by."

Deacon held his breath, watching as the door's keypad blinked from red to green. The lock disengaged with a faint hiss, and the door slid open, revealing the containment chamber beyond.

"Go, go, go," Hugo quietly urged, motioning them forward.

They slipped inside, their footsteps muffled by the thick carpeted floor. The room was dimly lit, the walls lined with shelves of odd, arcane objects. Strange artifacts, many of which Deacon couldn't begin to identify, filled the space. The fire alarm continued to echo faintly in the background, its wailing tone like a ticking clock counting down their time.

But in the center of the room, suspended in a glass case,

was what they'd come for: Eshu's Pendant.

Deacon's breath caught in his throat as he stared at it. The pendant seemed to pulse faintly, almost as if it were alive, its etched surface catching the light in a way that made it look almost... liquid.

He swallowed hard. "That's it."

"Yeah," Sean muttered, his gaze fixed on the pendant. "But we're not taking it, right?"

"Right," Hugo confirmed, his tone clipped. He reached into his jacket and pulled out a small black sensor. "We're just setting up the diversion."

Deacon nodded, moving to the far side of the room. He crouched beside a low shelf, carefully attaching the sensor to the underside. It emitted a soft, red glow before going dark.

"Sensor's in place," Deacon whispered, straightening.

"Good. Now let's move."

They turned to leave, but before they could take more than a few steps, a sudden, new blaring alarm filled the air—louder, more intense.

"Uh, that's not the fire alarm," Sean muttered, eyes wide.

"No," Hugo agreed, his voice tight. "It's not."

The door slid shut with a resounding thunk, locking them inside. Deacon's pulse raced as he glanced around, his mind scrambling for a solution.

"Delilah, we've got a problem," he hissed into his earpiece. "Containment room's sealed."

Static crackled in his ear, followed by Delilah's strained voice. "Von Heger must've activated a secondary lockout. Looks like he's on to your diversion. Hang tight, I've got Maria working on it."

Seconds stretched into what felt like an eternity as Deacon's gaze darted between the door and the pendant, the weight of their situation pressing down on him. With Von Heger onto their diversion plan, they would only have a few minutes before things really went south.

"We're running out of time," Sean whispered urgently. "What if—"

"Got it!" Delilah's triumphant voice cut through the tension. The door slid open, the lock disengaging.

"Move!" Hugo barked.

They slipped out of the containment chamber, the blaring alarm still echoing through the halls. Deacon's heart thundered in his chest as they ducked into a side corridor, their footsteps quick and silent.

"Von Heger's gonna know something's up," Deacon muttered breathlessly as they raced down the hallway.

"Exactly what we want him to think," Hugo replied grimly. "He'll move the pendant, just like we planned."

"Then we'll be ready," Sean added, a hint of determination in his voice.

They reached a narrow service passage, the door swinging open to reveal a stairwell leading down. Deacon glanced back, catching a glimpse of the containment chamber's lights flashing red.

"Delilah, you're up," Hugo said into his earpiece.

"Copy that," came her calm response. "They're already moving the convoy into position. Von Heger's taken the bait."

Deacon exchanged a quick glance with Sean, a surge of hope rising in his chest.

"Let's go," Hugo said, his voice firm. "We're not done yet."

Delilah leaned forward, her fingers tapping lightly against the console as she monitored the feed from the facility's exterior cameras. On one of the screens, the convoy's transport vehicles rumbled to life, engines growling as they prepared to move out.

"They're moving," she muttered to herself, a small smile tugging at her lips. "Just like we wanted."

She glanced at the live feed from the facility's internal cameras. Von Heger stood at the center of the chaos, issuing orders with a calm, authoritative air. But there was something in his posture—something tense, almost uncertain—that made her pulse quicken.

He knows something's wrong, she realized.

"Bixby, be ready," she said softly into her earpiece. "We're up next."

"Roger that," Bixby's voice crackled back, tinged with a mix of nerves and excitement. "I'm in position."

Delilah's eyes narrowed as she watched Von Heger step away from the convoy, his gaze sweeping the area one last time. For a split second, he seemed to hesitate.

"Don't second-guess yourself now, Von Heger," she murmured, a faint smile crossing her lips. "Everything's going exactly as planned."

With one last, lingering glance at the facility, Von Heger nodded sharply to his men. The convoy began to move.

And Delilah knew that, finally, the real heist was about to begin.

Von Heger's eyes narrowed as the last transport vehicle pulled away. "Hold it," he ordered sharply, his voice cutting through the air. His gaze swept over the facility's exterior, something unsettling gnawing at the back of his mind.

"Something's not right," he muttered, turning to one of his lieutenants. "Review the footage. I want to know exactly what happened in that containment chamber–and I want it now."

Chapter 35
The Pendant's Vulnerability

The low hum of the armored vehicle's engine vibrated through Von Heger's seat as the convoy rumbled away from the Order's research facility. He sat rigidly in the back seat, a leather-bound folder open on his lap and a tablet in hand. The glowing screen reflected off his narrowed eyes as he flicked through security logs and camera feeds, meticulously replaying the footage.

His fingers drummed absently against the armrest, a small tick that belied the calm facade he projected. Something gnawed at him—a feeling, a nagging whisper in the back of his mind that refused to be silenced. The Guardians were clever, no question, but this... this was almost too easy.

On the tablet, the replay of the facility's interior camera showed Deacon, Sean, and Hugo entering the containment chamber. They moved as expected, planting a sensor and setting off the fire alarm. Von Heger watched them step out, only for the feed to suddenly flicker—just a half-second distortion—before resuming.

His breath hitched, eyes narrowing. He rewound the footage

and leaned in closer. There it was again: a ghost image, a momentary glitch. But what caused it?

"Driver," Von Heger called out, his voice cool but commanding. "Slow the convoy. We may have a situation."

The agent in the passenger seat turned, his brow furrowing. "Sir?"

Von Heger didn't respond immediately. He scrolled through a few more logs, the small flickers in the data sparking a cold realization. Someone had been in the containment chamber before Deacon's group. Someone—or something—had tampered with the security feeds to hide it.

His gaze snapped up, lips pressing into a thin line. "Stop the vehicles. Now."

The agent's eyes widened, but he nodded and relayed the command. The convoy ground to a halt, tires crunching over gravel and asphalt as the armored vehicles came to a standstill on the side of the road.

Von Heger's hand tightened around the pendant case resting beside him. Could it be a trick within a trick? Had he underestimated Hugo and his team? He'd been so focused on capturing them that he hadn't considered what they might leave behind.

"Get me a status report on the containment chamber," he barked, voice edged with urgency. "I want to know if anything—anything—was altered."

"Right away, sir," the agent stammered, hurriedly typing into a small laptop mounted on the dashboard.

Von Heger's gaze remained fixed on the pendant case, the tiny latch securing it glinting faintly in the low light of the vehicle's interior. He had checked it before they left the facility, confirming that it was indeed the real pendant inside. And yet... The Guardians were notorious for playing the long game, for setting traps that didn't spring until their enemies were already caught.

His chest tightened as the agent looked up, face pale. "Sir, there's an anomaly in the containment logs. The security feed shows a duplicate access point—someone else accessed the chamber before we thought."

Von Heger's breath hissed out between clenched teeth. So, they had tampered with the pendant after all. "Deploy the response team. Sweep every vehicle in the convoy," he ordered sharply. "We're not moving another inch until I know exactly what's inside this case."

His fingers hovered over the latch of the pendant case, doubt swirling in his mind. Had they really pulled one over on him? Or was this just another distraction, meant to keep him off balance?

He didn't have time to second-guess. He flicked the small latch open.

The tension inside Delilah's vehicle was palpable. Bixby could feel it in the taut silence, in the way Delilah's eyes flicked back and forth between the road and the small radio sitting on the dashboard. He shifted in his seat, his hands twisting nervously in his lap.

"What's going on?" he whispered, glancing out the window. The convoy had stopped a few blocks away, the armored vehicles lined up like predators frozen in mid-pounce.

Delilah's gaze remained focused, calm and controlled. "Von Heger's realized something's wrong. He's checking the pendant."

Bixby's heart thudded in his chest, the adrenaline making his hands shake. "So… what do we do now?"

"We wait," Delilah murmured, her voice steady. "If he's as

paranoid as I think he is, he'll move it again. When he does, that's our moment."

Bixby swallowed hard, his mouth dry. He wasn't used to this—to sitting still, to waiting for someone else to make a move. But Delilah's presence, her quiet confidence, was grounding him in a way he hadn't expected.

The radio crackled softly, Von Heger's voice cutting through the static. "All units, prepare for immediate transport."

Delilah's lips curved into a small, satisfied smile. "There it is."

Bixby's pulse raced. "So… we're really going to do this?"

"Yes, Bixby," Delilah replied calmly, handing him a small radio. "When I give the signal, you pull our car out in front of the lead vehicle. Block their path. I'll handle the rest."

Bixby nodded, his grip tightening on the steering wheel. He took a deep breath, letting the air fill his lungs and steady his nerves. "Okay. I'm ready."

Delilah's eyes softened slightly, a hint of admiration flickering there. "Good. Remember—quick and precise. No heroics, no matter what."

"Got it," Bixby murmured, eyes narrowing as he watched the convoy begin to inch forward. His pulse thrummed in time with the engine's growl. This was his chance to prove himself—to show he was more than just a kid caught up in something way over his head.

The convoy picked up speed, rolling slowly down the empty street. Delilah's fingers brushed over the radio controls, her eyes locking onto the lead vehicle. "Now," she whispered.

Bixby's heart leapt into his throat as he slammed the gearshift into drive and pulled out into the road, tires squealing as the vehicle lurched forward. The convoy screeched to a halt, the drivers swerving to avoid a collision.

Delilah stepped out, her silhouette framed against the

headlights' glare. She raised her weapon, aiming it directly at the driver of the lead vehicle. "Step out of the car," she called, her voice calm but authoritative. "Now."

The driver hesitated, his gaze darting to the side mirrors, looking for guidance.

"I won't ask twice," Delilah warned, her stance steady.

Deacon crouched behind the dumpster, his breath coming in shallow bursts. He peered around the edge, his gaze locked on the unfolding scene in the middle of the street. The convoy was stalled, Delilah standing in the middle of the road like some kind of avenging angel.

"Come on, come on…" he muttered under his breath.

Beside him, Sean shifted anxiously, his eyes wide with anticipation. "This is it, right? The big moment?"

"Yeah," Deacon whispered, his heart pounding. "This is it."

He watched as Delilah and Bixby moved in perfect sync. The drivers, startled by Delilah's sudden appearance and the sight of Bixby's vehicle blocking the road, hesitated. And that was all they needed.

"Now!" Delilah shouted, her voice cutting through the night air like a knife.

The car doors flew open with a metallic clang as Delilah and Bixby moved with practiced precision. Delilah reached inside, her fingers brushing against the cool metal of the pendant case. She gripped it tightly and pulled it free, a thrill of victory coursing through her veins.

"Go, go, go!" she shouted, her voice cutting through the chaos.

Bixby didn't need to be told twice. He spun on his heel, sprinting back to their SUV. The sound of shouting and gunfire echoed behind them as Order agents scrambled to respond.

Delilah followed close on Bixby's heels, the pendant case clutched against her chest as if it were made of glass.

"Get in!" Bixby barked, throwing open the driver's side door and jumping behind the wheel. Delilah slid in beside him, slamming the door shut.

Bixby floored the accelerator. The tires squealed against the asphalt as the SUV shot forward, the engine roaring in protest. Deacon, Sean, and Hugo watched from their hiding spot behind a cluster of dumpsters as the vehicle careened down the road, weaving between the scattered Order agents.

"We did it," Sean whispered, disbelief and exhilaration mixing in his voice. "We actually did it!"

Deacon felt his heart lift, a smile beginning to spread across his face. They'd pulled it off—they'd gotten the pendant, and now they were getting out of here. For the first time since this whole mess had started, he felt a glimmer of hope.

But then Delilah's voice crackled through the earpiece, breathless and laced with something that sent a chill through Deacon's veins—uncertainty.

"Deacon, we've got a problem."

The smile died on Deacon's lips. "What? What's wrong?"

"The pendant case…" There was a pause, and Deacon could almost hear her racing heartbeat through the static. "It's empty. The pendant isn't here."

Silence fell like a lead weight. Deacon's mind raced, trying to process what she'd just said. The pendant wasn't there? But they'd planned for this—every step, every move. So why did it feel like something had gone horribly wrong?

"Von Heger," Hugo muttered, his expression dark. "He must have figured out our plan sooner than we thought. It was a setup. He's always one step ahead."

Deacon glanced back toward the road where the convoy was

now pulling away. The SUV carrying Delilah and Bixby sped off into the night, but as they reached the end of the block, a lone figure stepped into the street.

Von Heger.

He stood there, calm and composed, the streetlights casting long shadows around him. In his right hand, he held something small and dark, the metal catching the faint light in a way that sent a chill down Deacon's spine.

The pendant.

Von Heger's cold gaze locked onto them, and he lifted the pendant slightly, letting it dangle from his fingers. A triumphant smile curled his lips as if savoring every moment of their shock and confusion.

Deacon's heart skipped a beat. Von Heger wasn't supposed to have the pendant—fake or not. He was supposed to believe the one in the transport case was real. So why was he flaunting it like a trophy?

Did he know?

For a moment, everything hung in balance. Then Hugo's voice cut through the haze, sharp and controlled. "He's trying to rattle us. Stick to the plan. He doesn't know it's a fake."

Deacon nodded slowly, his pulse still racing. Of course. Von Heger couldn't know for sure. He was just being cautious, showing off in a way that only Von Heger would.

But it still meant he'd seen through at least part of their deception. And if that was true, then Delilah and Bixby were in even greater danger than they realized.

"Delilah," Hugo growled into his earpiece, his voice low and urgent. "It's a trap. Get out of there now."

But before Delilah could respond, Von Heger's voice cut through the night, crackling out of one of the Order radio units Hugo had picked up inside the facility. "Seize them," he ordered, his tone cold and measured. "The game is over."

Order agents swarmed the street, blocking every exit. The SUV skidded to a stop, trapped on all sides. Delilah and Bixby looked around wildly, but there was no way out. The trap had snapped shut.

From their hiding place, Deacon's heart sank as he watched the scene unfold. Von Heger had outmaneuvered them—again. He had the real pendant, and now Delilah and Bixby were surrounded.

Von Heger's gaze shifted, his eyes narrowing slightly as he stared directly at the alley where Deacon, Sean, and Hugo were hidden. For a heartbeat, Deacon thought he'd spotted them—but then Von Heger turned away, his focus returning to the pendant in his hand.

He lifted it slowly, his triumphant smile widening as he spoke, his voice calm and almost fatherly.

"Did you really think you could win?"

The words sent a chill down Deacon's spine. He felt the weight of their situation pressing down on him like a vise. The real pendant was still in Von Heger's possession, and now they were at his mercy.

"We need to move," Hugo whispered urgently, his eyes darting around as he calculated their next move. "We can't do anything for them right now. We have to regroup."

Deacon nodded numbly, his gaze still locked on Von Heger's triumphant form. They'd been so close. But Von Heger had been one step ahead the entire time.

"Let's go," he murmured, his voice hollow.

As they slipped away into the shadows, the sound of Von Heger's laughter echoed through the night, mingling with the distant wail of sirens. The Order agents closed in around the trapped SUV, weapons drawn, and Deacon forced himself to keep moving, even as the bitter taste of defeat filled his mouth.

The Order agents closed in, their weapons raised and faces set in grim determination. Delilah glanced around, assessing the situation. There was no way out. Not this time.

"Delilah?" Bixby's voice was tight with fear as he glanced at her. "What do we do?"

Delilah's jaw clenched, her gaze flickering between the agents and the narrow alleyway beside them. "We improvise," she murmured, her fingers brushing against the control panel. "Hang tight, Bixby."

Chapter 36
The Unmasking

Delilah's eyes narrowed as she watched the Order agents close in around them. There were too many to fight, and the streets offered no clear escape. But Delilah wasn't one to panic.

"Stay calm, Bixby," she murmured, keeping her gaze steady on the approaching agents. "I need you to trust me and drive like you've never driven before."

Bixby's knuckles whitened on the steering wheel. "Drive where? They've boxed us in—"

"Just do exactly what I say," she cut in, her voice cool and controlled. She glanced at him, catching his eye. "Can you do that?"

For a split second, Bixby hesitated. Then he gave a sharp nod, determination hardening his expression. "Yeah. I can."

"Good," Delilah said, her fingers flying over the control panel in front of her. A series of clicks echoed in the SUV's cabin as she activated the emergency protocols she'd built into the vehicle's systems. "On my mark, turn the wheel hard left and floor it."

"Left?" Bixby's eyes widened as he glanced at the narrow space between two parked cars. "But there's no—"

"Trust me," Delilah repeated, her voice a whisper of steel. She hit the final command, and the SUV's headlights flared blindingly bright, flooding the street with a searing white light. The agents staggered back, caught off guard.

"Now!" Delilah shouted.

Bixby didn't hesitate. He wrenched the wheel left, the tires screeching as the SUV surged forward. The vehicle squeezed through the narrow gap between the parked cars, the side mirrors barely missing the edges by a hair's breadth. A burst of adrenaline shot through Bixby as he swerved sharply, the SUV fishtailing slightly before he regained control.

"Go, go, go!" Delilah urged, her eyes darting to the side mirrors, watching the agents scramble in confusion.

The SUV shot down the side street, engines roaring as Bixby pushed the pedal to the floor. The Order agents' shouts faded into the background, and the sound of gunfire echoed behind them, but Bixby kept his focus forward, his gaze locked on the empty road ahead.

"We're clear," Delilah said, a faint smile of relief tugging at her lips. She glanced over at Bixby, admiration gleaming in her eyes. "You did good, Bixby. Really good."

Bixby let out a shaky breath, his grip on the steering wheel easing slightly. "Not bad for comic relief, huh?"

Delilah chuckled softly. "Not bad at all. Now let's get to the rendezvous point. Deacon and Hugo will need us."

With a quick, confident nod, Bixby guided the SUV through the darkened streets, leaving the Order agents behind as they sped off into the night.

Von Heger's fingers tapped an impatient rhythm against the

smooth leather of the armrest. The inside of the armored vehicle was dim, illuminated only by the faint glow of the tablet in his lap. He glanced at the screen again, eyes narrowed as he scrolled through the facility's security logs. The convoy moved smoothly along the deserted roads, their vehicles a steady procession of shadowy shapes in the night.

"Sir, the containment breach alert is still active," a voice crackled through his earpiece. "Should we continue to the rendezvous point or investigate further?"

Von Heger's eyes flicked up to the rearview monitor showing the transport vehicle ahead. The pendant was safely tucked away in a reinforced case, sealed and supposedly secured. But something about the entire situation was gnawing at him, an uneasy sensation that refused to dissipate.

"Hold position," he ordered sharply, the edge of his tone making the driver flinch. "I want a full diagnostic run on the pendant's containment status. Double-check for anomalies."

The driver hesitated, casting a worried glance toward the pendant's reinforced case visible through the rear compartment's bulletproof glass. "Sir... is something wrong?"

Von Heger's gaze returned to the tablet. He flicked through the security feeds again, each one displaying a different angle of the facility. There it was—Sector B, the containment wing. He watched Deacon and his group slip inside the chamber on the replay footage, exactly as he had expected them to. The fire alarm blaring, the guards scrambling to cover their flanks—everything had gone according to plan.

Yet... He rewound the footage, pausing at the moment Deacon attached a small black device under a shelf. It blinked faintly before going dark. A sensor? No, that was just a distraction. The real trick was elsewhere. Something felt off. Too simple. Too neat.

"Diagnostic shows no physical breach," the driver's voice interrupted his thoughts, sounding relieved. "The containment seal remains intact."

"No physical breach, no." Von Heger's voice was a low murmur as he zoomed in on the screen. Then he noticed it—a subtle flicker on one of the feeds. The tiniest of glitches, almost imperceptible to the naked eye. He rewound it again, playing the segment in slow motion. There it was, the briefest ghost image—a blurred shadow passing through the chamber's doorway before Deacon and his group had even arrived.

His breath hitched as realization crashed over him like a icy wave.

"Stop the convoy!" he barked, his voice cutting through the air like a whip. The vehicle lurched to a sudden halt, the driver glancing back at him in confusion. "Get me the pendant. Now!"

Two Order agents scrambled to comply, the rear door swinging open as they rushed to retrieve the reinforced case. Von Heger's eyes never left the monitor. The ghost image had been deliberate—a trick played on him. The logs had been altered.

"They didn't come for the pendant," he muttered, his voice filled with disbelief and mounting fury. "They came to make me move it. To make me believe they were coming for it." Rage began building inside him like a wave, swelling with each moment of clarity.

The reinforced case was brought forward, and Von Heger snatched it with almost feral intensity. His fingers trembled slightly as he punched in the access code. The case beeped softly, its locks disengaging with a faint hiss. He lifted the lid, revealing the pendant nestled within.

It looked perfect. Unblemished. Identical to the real one.

Except... it wasn't.

Von Heger stared at the pendant, the blood draining from his face. A faint trace of energy, something only someone with his training and sensitivity could detect, emanated from the artifact. It felt different—wrong. The energy signature was off, a fabricated copy of the real thing. It was a fake.

His hand tightened around the pendant, his knuckles whitening with suppressed rage. "No..." he whispered, his voice deadly soft. "No!" He forced himself to steady his breathing. He couldn't let his men see his loss of control from the rage boiling inside.

The driver flinched at the tone, eyes widening. "Sir...?"

Von Heger's gaze snapped to him, and the driver recoiled as if struck. "It's a decoy. The real pendant is still at the facility. Turn the convoy around. We're going back."

"But... but sir, the rendezvous—"

"NOW!" Von Heger roared, the force of his voice reverberating through the vehicle. The driver slammed the gearshift, and the convoy swerved, engines roaring as they tore back down the road toward the facility.

Von Heger's fingers drummed furiously against the side of the case. "You think you're clever, don't you?" he whispered, his voice seething with fury. "But you've underestimated me. You won't leave that facility alive, Deroche. None of you will."

Bixby's hands trembled on the steering wheel, his knuckles barely maintaining their grip. He cast a quick, restless glance at Delilah, then back at the narrow street ahead. The SUV was wedged awkwardly between a low stone wall and a thick row of hedges, the leafy branches pressing up against the windows like fingers trying to reach inside. His heart still pounded in his ears, each beat a reminder of the sheer insanity they'd just escaped. He took a shaky breath, trying to steady his nerves, but every muscle in his body seemed locked in a frantic attempt to either take off at full speed or just completely shut down.

"Delilah, what... what happens now?" he asked, his voice tight and pitched higher than usual, the adrenaline coursing through his veins refusing to fade.

Delilah's eyes were fixed on the feed from the hidden camera she'd planted on the convoy's route. Her expression was calm, almost serene, but Bixby knew better. There was a razor's edge of intensity beneath that calm exterior.

"Von Heger's figured out the pendant is a fake," she murmured. "He's turning back."

"What?" Bixby's eyes widened. "But that's good, right? We wanted him to—"

"Not this soon," Delilah cut in, her gaze sharpening. "We needed more time to finish the extraction. He's going to double back to the facility and catch Hugo and Deacon before they can get out."

Panic flared in Bixby's chest. "So... what do we do?"

Delilah's lips curved into a small, dangerous smile. "We intercept him. If we can delay him long enough, the others can complete the mission."

Bixby swallowed hard, his palms slick with sweat. "Intercept Von Heger? Again? I mean, I'm a cornerback on my High School football team. I intercept bad passes...not bad guys. You've got to be kidding, right?"

"Do I look like I'm kidding?" Delilah's voice was soft but firm. She handed him the radio, her gaze steady. "You're the wheelman, remember? You get us in and out, no questions asked. Think you can handle that?"

Bixby took the radio, his fingers trembling slightly. He looked at Delilah, then back at the convoy on the screen. "I-I think so," he stammered at first, but then, with a deep breath, he steadied himself. "Yeah, I can handle it."

Delilah's smile widened, a glint of approval in her eyes. "Good. Now, get us into position. We've got a convoy to stop."

Deacon's breath puffed in the cold night air as he crouched behind the low concrete wall of the facility's rooftop. The lights of the city stretched out before him, but his focus was entirely on the courtyard below. He watched through the binoculars as the Order's transport convoy skidded to a halt, guards spilling out in a flurry of activity.

"They're already back," he whispered, voice tinged with worry.

Hugo's voice was a low growl beside him. "Von Heger knows. He's coming for the real pendant."

Sean glanced between them, his brow furrowed. "But we've got it, right? We're ahead of him?"

Deacon nodded slowly. "Yeah... but if he catches us, it won't matter. He's too close."

"So, what do we do?" Sean asked, his voice rising slightly.

Deacon took a deep breath, his gaze flicking to the pendant in his hand—the real one, glowing faintly in the dim light. He smiled inwardly, remembering the split-second switch they'd made back in the confusion of Sector B. Von Heger had seen exactly what they wanted him to see. He tucked it carefully into the hidden compartment in his jacket.

"We stick to the plan," Deacon said firmly, his voice steadier than he felt. "We get out. Delilah and Bixby will buy us time. We just have to trust them."

He glanced back at the transport vehicles below, Von Heger's furious shouts echoing through the night.

"Whatever happens," Deacon whispered, "we don't let him win."

The three of them rose, moving silently toward the far edge of the rooftop, ready to make their escape.

"Ready?" Hugo murmured, his gaze never leaving the courtyard.

Deacon nodded, heart hammering. "Ready."

And with that, they vanished into the night, the real heist still unfolding beneath Von Heger's unsuspecting gaze.

Chapter 37
The Great Escape

A biting wind whipped across the rooftop, rattling loose gravel underfoot as Deacon, Sean, and Hugo crouched behind the low concrete wall. The darkened courtyard below was a hive of activity, guards moving like shadows as their radios crackled with terse commands. A row of transport vehicles sat idling near the facility's main gate, their headlights slicing through the darkness.

Deacon's gaze darted to the pendant in his hand, its faint glow barely visible in the predawn light. It felt almost surreal—after everything they'd been through, he was holding it in his grasp. The very thing that had put them all in danger. The very thing Von Heger was desperate to control.

"Deacon," Sean whispered, his breath clouding in the chill air. "What now?"

Deacon glanced at Hugo, who nodded toward a metal access ladder bolted to the side of the building. It led down to a narrow ledge that ran along the building's second story—close enough to the ground to jump from without breaking anything, if they landed right.

"We get down there," Hugo murmured, nodding toward the narrow ledge that ran along the side of the building, leading to a shadowed section of the courtyard. "Stay low and move when I say."

The wind gusted around them, carrying the faint sounds of shouts and the distant blare of the facility's still-blaring fire alarm. Deacon's heart pounded in his ears as he waited, watching the guards' movements. Everything hinged on their timing.

"Now!" Hugo hissed.

They slipped over the edge, gripping the rungs of the ladder as they made their descent. The metal was cold and slick under Deacon's hands, the smell of rust sharp and acrid. He bit back a wince, focusing on keeping his footing steady. Sean was just ahead of him, moving carefully but quickly. One wrong move, and they'd be spotted—or worse, fall.

Reaching the ledge, Deacon crouched low, pressing himself flat against the wall. His pulse hammered as he glanced down at the narrow gap below, a drop that seemed to stretch forever despite only being a couple of meters.

"Okay, easy now," he whispered to himself. "Just like Bob taught you..."

He swung over the edge and dropped. The impact jarred his knees, but he rolled with the momentum, coming up in a crouch beside Sean. Hugo landed beside them a moment later, his gaze snapping up to the rooftop above.

"We're good," Hugo murmured. "Let's move."

They crept along the ledge, keeping to the shadows. The guards below were still clustered around the transport vehicles, oblivious to their presence. Deacon's heart raced as they reached the far end of the ledge, where a drainpipe ran down to the ground below.

"One at a time," Hugo instructed, glancing at Sean. "You

first."

Sean hesitated, then nodded, gripping the drainpipe and shimmying down. The metal groaned slightly under his weight, but he made it to the ground without incident. Deacon followed, his scraped fingers screaming in protest as he slid down. He hit the ground and crouched low, scanning the courtyard for any signs of movement.

"Come on," he breathed, willing Hugo to hurry.

A faint metallic click echoed across the rooftop, followed by a soft hum that sent a shiver down Deacon's spine. He looked up, eyes widening as red lights began to flash along the building's exterior.

"What is that?" Sean whispered, his voice tight with panic.

"Lockdown protocol," Hugo muttered as he dropped down beside them, his expression grim. "Von Heger's sealed the exits. He knows we're trying to get out."

Deacon's stomach lurched. "So, what do we do?"

"We improvise," Hugo said, his voice firm. "Follow me."

Delilah adjusted the focus on her night vision binoculars, tracking Deacon and the others as they moved along the facility's perimeter. The flashing red lights reflected off the courtyard's metal fencing, casting eerie shadows across the ground. She could see Von Heger's men scrambling to cover the exits, their shouts barely audible over the crackling of the facility's PA system.

"They're sealing everything up," Delilah murmured into her earpiece, her voice calm despite the tension thrumming through her. "You need to keep moving, stay out of sight."

"We're working on it," Hugo's voice crackled back. "Any sign of our exit?"

Delilah glanced at the SUV's dashboard, where a digital map

displayed a live feed of the facility's security grid. Her fingers flew over the controls, disabling a few more cameras to clear their path.

"South side is still open," she replied. "But you'll need to get across the main courtyard. They're putting up barriers."

"Understood," Hugo said shortly.

Delilah's gaze flicked to Bixby, who was hunched over the steering wheel, his eyes darting between the side mirrors and the narrow alleyway. His fingers tapped a nervous rhythm against the dashboard, his knuckles pale.

"You okay?" she asked softly, her tone gentler than usual.

Bixby swallowed hard, his Adam's apple bobbing. "Yeah, I just... We're really gonna get them out of there, right?"

"Of course we are," Delilah said firmly, giving him a reassuring smile. "Just be ready. We might need to move fast."

A flicker of movement caught her eye, and she turned back to the binoculars. A group of guards was converging on a side entrance—Von Heger's secondary team.

"Bixby," Delilah murmured, her gaze narrowing. "We've got company."

Von Heger's fingers danced across the console, his eyes locked on the monitors as he pulled up every camera feed in the facility. The red lights flashing across the screens only heightened his focus. He could see them—Deacon and his group—moving along the southern perimeter, slipping past his guards with frustrating ease.

"Block all southern exits," he ordered, his voice a low growl. "I want that courtyard locked down tight."

"Yes, sir," one of the agents responded, typing furiously at the control station.

Von Heger leaned closer to the screen, his eyes narrowing.

He watched Deacon drop down from the wall, landing silently in the shadows. There was something infuriatingly calm about their movements, as if they weren't running for their lives but executing a well-rehearsed routine.

They think they're going to get away, he thought, a slow smile spreading across his face. But they've forgotten one thing.

He reached for the command console and keyed in the lockdown protocol. A series of heavy, metallic clunks echoed through the facility as blast doors slammed shut, sealing off every exit.

"Got you," Von Heger whispered.

He watched with satisfaction as Deacon and his group froze, looking around in confusion. Then they started moving again, faster this time, slipping through the narrow gap between two of the vehicles.

"Try all you want, Mr. Koster," Von Heger murmured. "But this time, you're not going anywhere."

Deacon's lungs burned as he sprinted across the courtyard, his eyes darting from shadow to shadow. The red lights flashed in sync with the pounding of his heart, the lockdown alarms blaring in his ears.

"Keep going!" Hugo barked, his voice cutting through the noise. "We're almost there!"

A shout rang out from behind them—guards. Deacon glanced back, his breath catching as he saw the group of armed men rushing toward them, their weapons raised.

"Hugo!" he shouted, pointing.

"Don't stop!" Hugo growled, his pace never faltering. "We just need to get over the wall. Delilah's waiting on the other side."

Sean stumbled, his foot catching on a loose piece of gravel.

Deacon grabbed his arm, hauling him upright. "Come on!" he urged, his voice strained.

They reached the wall, a high concrete barrier that loomed above them like an insurmountable fortress. Deacon's heart sank. It was higher than he'd expected—too high to scale without some serious help.

Hugo didn't hesitate. He dropped to one knee, lacing his fingers together. "Go!" he ordered.

Deacon swallowed hard and stepped onto Hugo's hands. With a grunt, Hugo heaved him upward. Deacon's hands scrabbled against the rough concrete, his muscles straining as he pulled himself up. He swung his leg over the top and crouched there, reaching back down.

"Sean, grab my hand!" he called, his voice tight with urgency.

Sean hesitated, glancing nervously over his shoulder as the sound of approaching footsteps echoed through the courtyard. He nodded, then took a deep breath and jumped off of Hugo offered hands. Deacon caught his wrist, gritting his teeth as he hauled Sean up beside him. They both teetered precariously on the narrow ledge, breaths coming in harsh gasps.

"Hugo, your turn!" Deacon shouted.

Hugo jumped, his powerful arms latching onto the top of the wall. Deacon and Sean grabbed him under the shoulders, straining to pull him up. For a moment, it seemed like they wouldn't be able to lift him, but then Hugo gave a final push with his legs, and he clambered over the top, collapsing beside them.

Just as Hugo caught his breath, a spotlight swept across the wall, bathing them in harsh white light. "There they are!" a guard shouted, and the crack of gunfire split the air.

"Get down!" Deacon yelled, ducking as bullets chipped and flaked the concrete around them. He glanced down at the other side of the wall—just a short drop to the ground below. Without hesitating, he swung over the edge and dropped.

Sean and Hugo followed, landing in the dirt beside him with grunts of pain. Deacon winced as his battered knees absorbed the impact. More bullets cracked into the wall, turning what had been an obstacle into their only cover.

"Go, go, go!" Hugo urged, his voice a low growl.

They sprinted across the narrow alley, feet pounding against the pavement, the SUV's engine a low, reassuring hum in the dark. As they reached the vehicle, Delilah's voice crackled through their earpieces. "Get in!"

They dove into the vehicle, the doors slamming shut behind them. Bixby's foot hit the gas, and the SUV shot forward, tires screeching as they peeled out of the alley.

The SUV barreled down the street, Deacon glancing back at the shrinking facility behind them. In the light spilling from the entryway to the courtyard, a dark silhouette stood outlined against the flashing lights—Von Heger. For now, they were free—but what came next was anyone's guess.

Chapter 38
Homecoming

Von Heger's fingers trembled with barely suppressed rage as he watched the security footage on the screens before him. The control room was silent, every agent within it holding their breath as the Order's leader reviewed the altered logs.

He rewound the footage for what felt like the hundredth time, his eyes narrowing as he replayed the scene in slow motion. There it was again—the brief, flickering ghost image of someone accessing the containment chamber before Deacon's group had even entered the facility. It was subtle, almost imperceptible, but unmistakable now that he knew what to look for.

Von Heger's jaw clenched, his teeth grinding audibly. "How could I have missed it..." he muttered under his breath, his voice low and dangerous.

He tapped a command into the console, isolating the timestamp of the breach. The system had been expertly manipulated— But who could have orchestrated this? The kids had talent, but this... this was the work of someone operating on an entirely different level. They hadn't just bypassed his security—they'd rewritten his reality, made him see what they wanted him to see.

"They planned every move," he murmured, his tone almost contemplative. "They led me right to it."

Von Heger straightened, his shoulders tense as he turned to the agents stationed behind him. They flinched under his steely gaze, the air around him charged with an almost palpable fury.

"Recall our forces," he ordered, his voice like ice. "Pull back and initiate a full diagnostic of all systems. I want every log, every file, every piece of data reviewed. Find out exactly when the breach happened and who was involved."

The agents scrambled to comply, their fingers flying over the keyboards.

"And one more thing," Von Heger added softly, his gaze drifting back to the screen showing Deacon's face as he slipped out of the facility. "Mark this day. The Koster family has cost us before, but never like this." His lips twisted into a snarl. "This boy… he's different. He's reckless, unpredictable. But he's also resourceful and clever. Those two traits make him more dangerous than any Guardian I've yet come across."

A dark smile curled at the corners of Von Heger's mouth, a plan already forming in his mind. "Prepare for a long engagement, gentlemen," he whispered, almost to himself. "The young Koster and his merry band may think they've won the game, but they've only just begun to play."

He turned sharply, his coat swirling behind him like a shadow. "When I strike next, I will not be playing by the same rules."

And with that, he strode out of the control room, leaving his men to carry out his orders. This wasn't over. Not by a long shot.

The dark woods outside the city limits blurred into shadows as Bixby pushed the SUV's engine to its limit. Inside the vehicle, silence lay heavy over the group. The adrenaline still pulsed through Deacon's veins, his heart pounding in time with the rumble of the tires on the gravel road. But as the headlights pierced through the dense underbrush, casting fleeting glimpses of gnarled trees and overgrown paths, the intensity of their escape began to fade, leaving behind an uneasy quiet. This was the calm after the storm—the fragile lull where the weight of what they had done settled like a heavy shroud.

The cabin's warmth enveloped Deacon like a blanket as he stepped inside, the chill of the night still lingering on his skin. The group trudged into the living room, exhaustion pulling at their limbs, but the sense of relief and triumph was palpable.

"Everyone okay?" Hugo asked, his voice rough as he glanced around the room. He still had a fierce, alert look in his eyes, as if expecting an enemy to burst through the door at any moment.

"More or less," Sean mumbled, sinking onto the couch. He leaned his head back, eyes closed. "Just... need a minute."

"Take your time," Hugo said, clapping Sean on the shoulder. He turned to Deacon, his gaze steady. "You did good out there."

Deacon nodded, but his mind was elsewhere. His fingers brushed against the pendant tucked safely in his pocket, the weight of it seeming to increase with each passing second. He glanced at Delilah, who was watching him with an unreadable expression.

"This thing..." he began, pulling the pendant out and holding it up. The faint glow seemed to pulse in time with his heartbeat. "What are we supposed to do with it now? I mean, what does it even mean?"

Delilah stepped forward, her gaze lingering on the pendant before shifting back to Deacon's eyes. "Eshu's Pendant is more than just an artifact. It's a symbol of power, influence—something the Order would use to tip the scales in their favor. Keeping it away from them was the right choice, but it's not the end of the fight. There are others like it, Deacon. Other artifacts, other battles."

"So, it's a never-ending war?" Bixby asked, his voice soft but steady. "One thing after another?"

"Not exactly," Hugo said, folding his arms across his chest. "We're not trying to win a war. We're just trying to keep the balance. Make sure people like Von Heger don't send the world into chaos." Hugo's gaze was distant, his fingers tapping an irregular rhythm against his leg. "I should've been there that day. Tecumseh called me for backup—said he had a lead on Eshu's Pendant. I was delayed, tied up with a mess Von Heger's people made in North Africa. They targeted a refugee camp, killed innocent people, just to keep me away." His voice dropped, a growl of restrained fury. "By the time I arrived, Cump was dead. Von Heger was gone. I've been chasing them both ever since."

"That's why you—" Deacon started, but Hugo cut him off with a sharp nod.

"That's why I won't let it happen again. No more delays, no more loose ends." He shot a hard look at Deacon. "And why I need you in this, kid. This fight—it's bigger than any of us. But it's personal, too."

Deacon's throat tightened as Hugo's words sank in—this wasn't just a mission; it was a reckoning. He glanced at each of them, seeing the fatigue and resolve etched into their faces. It struck him then that each person here wasn't fighting for glory or recognition—they were fighting to protect what they loved. He looked down at the pendant, turning it over in his hand. He could feel its pull—like a gravity well, drawing him in. He thought of everything they'd been through to get it, everything they'd risked. And now… what?

"I don't know if I can do this," he whispered, more to

himself than anyone else. "Be part of... whatever this is. The Guardians, this fight. It's so much bigger than me."

Hugo stepped closer, his expression softening. "You don't have to decide now. Just know there's a place for you here—if you want it."

Deacon swallowed hard, his gaze flicking to each of them—Hugo, Sean, Delilah, Bixby, even Maria. All of them had put their lives on the line for this. For him.

Deacon stared at the pendant in his hand, its surface glinting faintly in the low light. It felt heavier than it should have, like a chain tying him to something he didn't fully understand. He wanted to hold onto it, to keep it safe himself—but that desire tangled with fear, like vines choking a young sapling, threatening to crush him under the weight of expectation. If he gave it up, was he just walking away from everything his uncle had stood for? Or was he finally freeing himself from a destiny he wasn't ready for?

Taking a deep breath, he held out the pendant to Hugo. "Take it," he said quietly. "For now. I need... time."

Hugo accepted the pendant with a solemn nod, tucking it away. "We'll be here, Deacon. Whenever you're ready."

Ashebridge, North Carolina

The cabin's front door creaked open, and Mr. Oliver's voice carried through the living room. "Well, I was beginning to wonder if you lot had gotten lost."

Deacon turned, surprise flickering across his face. "Mr. Oliver?"

Mr. Oliver raised an eyebrow, looking pointedly at Bixby. "I'm assuming you have an explanation as to why you've been gone so long? And... where's your car?"

Bixby winced. "Um, about that... There was this deer,

or—no, actually it was a stag, a big one. Thing came out of nowhere!"

"Totaled it," Sean added helpfully from his spot on the couch, eyes still closed. "It was spectacular."

Hugo cleared his throat. "My company will take care of it. Insurance will cover everything."

Mr. Oliver looked between them all, a slow smile spreading across his face. "I suppose I shouldn't expect anything less from you boys." He nodded to Hugo. "Thank you for your generosity. And gentlemen—school starts back in two weeks. You're already enrolled. I trust that won't be a problem?"

Deacon and Sean exchanged a look, grinning despite themselves. "No problem, sir," Deacon said.

"Good." Mr. Oliver turned to leave, pausing at the door. "Welcome back. And... well done."

Watching Mr. Oliver leave, Sean turned to Deacon, "Jeesh, we just saved the world and now they want us to worry about algebra?"

"I think you can handle a little math," Deacon laughed.

Delilah leaned against the wall, watching the boys laugh and relax, a small smile on her lips. She knew there was more ahead for all of them, but for now, this was enough.

Sean wandered through the cabin, rubbing his stomach absentmindedly. "There's gotta be snacks somewhere around here..." He pulled open a few cabinets, finding nothing but dust. With a sigh, he pushed against one panel, expecting more emptiness—only for it to swing inward, revealing a hidden staircase.

"What the..." Sean muttered, his eyes widening. "Another one of these?"

Curiosity flaring, he slipped inside, descending the narrow

steps. The air grew cooler, and the sound of machinery hummed faintly. He reached the bottom, stepping into a sprawling underground lair that made his jaw drop.

High-tech equipment lined the walls—computers, surveillance systems, communications gear. Maps marked with red and blue pins spread out across a massive table in the center. It was a command center, fully equipped and operational. An area with gym equipment and martial arts training gear was set off in one corner. A shooting range with a veritable arsenal of weapons occupied another.

"Deacon!" he called, his voice echoing. "You gotta see this!"

Deacon appeared moments later, his eyes widening as he took in the scene. "Whoa…"

"Yeah," Sean breathed, a grin spreading across his face. "Your uncle… I think he was like Batman."

Deacon chuckled but stared at the maps, a strange look crossing his face as he walked over to one. "What were you preparing for, Uncle Cump?" His fingers brushed against a leather-bound journal sitting on the table, worn with age. He flipped it open, the familiar scrawl of his uncle's handwriting filling the page.

> *"The Guardians were formed at a turning point in history,"* the entry read. *"Constantine the Great's dream was to preserve knowledge against the chaos of a crumbling empire. What began as a simple task—to guard the accumulated wisdom of Rome—evolved as new threats emerged. The Order's rise forced us to change, to defend not just knowledge but the balance of power. It's a struggle that's taken us across centuries, across continents. And now, I fear we're on the verge of losing it all."*

Deacon swallowed, his heart pounding as he scanned the pages. His uncle's notes were filled with details of secret meetings, alliances forged and broken, operations that spanned the globe. Cump had been trying to find a way to strike back—to uncover the Order's hidden network. But his last entry ended abruptly, the final words smeared and unfinished:

> *"There's something more. Something buried in—"*

Deacon stood at the center of the lair, staring at the maps marked with Order strongholds and Guardian safehouses. He glanced at Sean, who grinned with that eager, ready-for-anything expression.

Deacon's gaze shifted to Delilah, who had joined them. "So," he murmured, his voice steady. "What's next?"

Delilah smiled. "That's up to you. But just know— Whatever comes next, we'll be ready. So… what's it going to be, Deacon?"

Epilogue

Washington, D.C.

The mahogany-paneled room was dimly lit, the soft glow of a single chandelier casting long shadows across the polished floor. Heavy velvet drapes muted the sounds of the bustling city outside, turning the chamber into a world of quiet power and secrecy. A large mahogany desk dominated the space, its surface immaculate except for a single crystal decanter and two tumblers.

Von Heger stood rigidly in the center of the room, his gloved hands clasped behind his back. He kept his gaze steady, staring straight ahead as if he were addressing a commanding officer on a battlefield. The fury that simmered beneath his calm facade was masked by years of discipline and self-control, but a keen observer would have noticed the slight tightening of his jaw, the rigidness of his posture.

"Sit," a voice said from behind the desk, low and steady, with the weight of authority that brooked no disobedience.

Von Heger lowered himself into the leather-backed chair, his movements precise and controlled. The figure seated opposite him leaned back in his chair, fingers steepled under his chin as

229

he studied Von Heger with cold, calculating eyes. This man's presence was palpable, a quiet intensity that seemed to fill every corner of the room.

"You failed to retrieve Eshu's Pendant." It wasn't a question. It was a statement of fact, delivered without a hint of emotion.

Von Heger inclined his head slightly, acknowledging the truth. "Yes, sir. The pendant slipped through our grasp due to a series of unforeseen interferences."

The man's gaze did not waver. He was older, his pale features sharp and angular, with a neatly trimmed beard that gave him an almost regal appearance. He exuded an aura of quiet menace, the kind that came from decades—centuries, perhaps—of commanding absolute loyalty and obedience.

"And yet," the man continued, his voice softer now, almost contemplative, "you had the boy within your reach. You were so certain of your victory, were you not?"

A flicker of irritation crossed Von Heger's face, but he quickly suppressed it. "We underestimated him," he admitted, his tone cold. "The Koster boy is more resourceful than we anticipated. He possesses a reckless courage that makes him unpredictable. He's clever, willing to take risks others would balk at."

"Yes," the man murmured, his gaze sharpening. "It seems we've been caught off guard by this new generation of Guardians. But no matter. The pendant is of little consequence in the grand scheme of things. There are other artifacts, other ways to achieve our goals."

Von Heger's jaw tightened imperceptibly. "With respect, sir, the pendant's power—"

"—is not the only power we possess," the man interrupted smoothly, his eyes locking onto Von Heger's with a glint of something dangerous. "Nor is it the only weapon at our disposal.

The Guardians' meddling will not go unchecked."

A heavy silence settled over the room, broken only by the faint ticking of an ornate clock on the wall. Von Heger remained still, waiting.

"Redouble our efforts in the other operations," the man ordered, his voice a low, resonant command. "Increase surveillance on all known Guardian strongholds. Strengthen our ties with those sympathetic to our cause. And most importantly..." He leaned forward, the shadows deepening the creases of his stern face. "Begin preparations for a full-scale engagement. We've allowed these interferences for too long. After fifteen hundred years of obstruction, it's time the Guardians were eliminated once and for all."

Von Heger inclined his head once more, a spark of dark satisfaction lighting his eyes. "It will be done."

The man leaned back again, his gaze distant as if he were already envisioning the coming conflict. "The boy—this Deacon Koster—he's shown he has potential. A dangerous kind of potential. We need to ensure he never realizes it."

Von Heger's lips twisted into a cold smile. "I'll see to it personally. Next time, there will be no escape."

"Good," the man said softly, his voice like a serpent's hiss. "We cannot afford to let the Guardians think they've gained the upper hand. Let them have their victory for now, but make no mistake..." His eyes darkened, the air in the room seeming to chill with his next words. "We will break them."

Von Heger rose smoothly, bowing his head in respect. "I will begin at once. The Guardians will learn what it means to challenge us."

The man watched as Von Heger turned and strode from the room, his movements once again precise and controlled. As the door clicked shut, he reached for the crystal decanter, pouring himself a measure of dark, amber liquid. He swirled the contents thoughtfully, his gaze fixed on the space where Von Heger had stood.

"The boy," he murmured softly to himself, a slow, calculating smile spreading across his lips. "So full of fire and defiance. But fire can be extinguished… and defiance can be broken."

He lifted the tumbler to his lips, savoring the burn as he drank deeply. The Guardians had been a thorn in their side for centuries, always resisting, always protecting. But now, with the rise of this new generation, the stakes had changed. And so, too, would the Order's response.

The man set the tumbler down with a soft clink, his fingers tapping a slow rhythm against the polished wood of the desk.

"Enjoy your moment of triumph, young Koster," he whispered, his voice barely more than a breath. "Because it will be your last."

About the Author

Benjamin Hines

Benjamin Hines is a native of North Georgia with a restless soul who somehow always finds his way home to the mountains. He writes stories for the people he loves and hopes others will enjoy them, too. When he is not traveling the world working towards a more sustainable future, he can be found with his family at their home just north of Atlanta or at the family farm nestled in the foothills of the Appalachians.

Made in the USA
Columbia, SC
25 October 2024

45055460R00145